## "Ballard?"

He blinked as he heard his name on her lips, recovering quickly from his momentary speechlessness as he stared at her.

"A good-night kiss," he whispered, moving in closer.

Her open palms immediately came to his chest, pushing slightly against him. He was certain it was to stop him. The problem was that it hadn't reached her eyes. Instead, as Ballard looked at Janelle, he saw her lips parting slightly, her tongue snaking out to lick the bottom one then retreating inside quickly as she cleared her throat.

"Yes," he began, reaching a hand up to rub the back of his fingers along her cheekbone and down the line of her jaw. "You can agree because you want to. Or you can simply tell me no, and I'll leave."

She hesitated, her hands still on his chest, making his desire burn hotter. After another second or so of indecision, her lips parted once more, and a small sound escaped.

"Ye—" she began to say.

And Ballard moved in, swooping his lips down over hers, taking the plumpness into his mouth before pressing his tongue inside.

She replied hungrily, grabbing the lapels of his jacket tightly in her fingers, tilting her head slightly so that when he deepened the kiss she was more than ready.

## Books by A.C. Arthur

Harlequin Kimani Romance

*Love Me Like No Other*
*A Cinderella Affair*
*Guarding His Body*
*Second Chance, Baby*
*Defying Desire*
*Full House Seduction*
*Summer Heat*
*Sing Your Pleasure*
*Touch of Fate*
*Winter Kisses*
*Desire a Donovan*
*Surrender to a Donovan*
*Decadent Dreams*
*Eve of Passion*

---

## A.C. ARTHUR

was born and raised in Baltimore, Maryland, where she currently resides with her husband and three children. An active imagination and a love for reading encouraged her to begin writing in high school, and she hasn't stopped since.

Working in the legal field for almost thirteen years, she's seen lots of horrific things and longs for the safe haven reading a romance novel brings. Determined to bring a new edge to romance, she continues to develop intriguing plots, sensual love scenes, racy characters and fresh dialogue—thus keeping readers on their toes!

For all the latest news on A.C. Arthur's books, giveaways, appearances and discussions, join A.C.'s Book Lounge on Facebook.

# *Eve*
### *of*
# *Passion*

## A.C. ARTHUR

HARLEQUIN® KIMANI™ ROMANCE

To all the newlyweds, make every moment count!

Recycling programs
for this product may
not exist in

3 1967 01349 0977

ISBN-13: 978-0-373-86374-7

EVE OF PASSION

**H HARLEQUIN**®
™ www.Harlequin.com

**Printed in U.S.A.**

Dear Reader,

One of my favorite hobbies is event planning. So imagine my elation when I was asked to write this story about Janelle Howerton, an event planner! I absolutely love weddings and have planned a few in my time. Writing about Janelle's hard-won trip down the aisle was a tremendous pleasure.

Janelle and Ballard were a special couple in that they both had high ideals for themselves and expectations neither of them could possibly meet—not alone, anyway. As they traveled the path to love, I felt a sense of pride at their personal growth and cheered them on every step of the way. I hope you, too, will root for this couple as they discover that no amount of material possessions or career achievements could make up for loving someone and being loved equally in return.

A.C. Arthur

# Prologue

"You did not just say Justin Bieber," Sandra Woolcott exclaimed after setting her wineglass down as gently as she could manage.

Vicki Ahlfors chuckled and shook her head.

"Yes, that's what I said," Janelle Howerton replied. "Or rather, that's what the Parents' Association secretary had typed on the list of demands they presented me this afternoon. In their words, 'it is imperative that this year's event have a wow factor.'"

"And Justin Bieber is a wow factor?" Sandra asked, still looking as if she just could not wrap her mind around the committee's suggestion.

"Justin Bieber is a 'wow, look what he's doing now' factor," Vicki offered. "The last thing we need in Wintersage is the press and those no-class tabloid people hanging around reporting Bieber's dirt and mixing it in with our homegrown dirt."

Janelle nodded. "I absolutely concur. We have enough going here in Wintersage to write a couple of tell-all books. Besides, I'm thinking of classier entertainment."

"Well, I guess by *wow factor,* they must mean who's hot in the music industry right now. You could get Rihanna," Vicki suggested.

"I never did understand why the town put so much time and money into a homecoming dance," Sandra said. "It's a high school function, not a national holiday."

Janelle tapped a glossy peach-painted nail against her glass, partially agreeing with Sandra's last comments. It was only a high school dance, but just about every adult living in Wintersage had attended Wintersage Academy, and thus all of them, the mayor and her director of finance included, thought this was the biggest event of the fall season. And since they'd already paid half Janelle's commission to plan the event, she had no choice but to go along with their madness.

"Do you remember the homecoming dances when we went to Wintersage? They were the best parties of the school year," Janelle recollected.

She, Sandra and Vicki had attended Wintersage Academy together and had even gone on to Nillson University in North Carolina as a trio. When their career dreams seemed as in sync as every other aspect of their lives, they'd opened The Silk Sisters, a one-stop shop for the most over-the-edge, sophisticated and creative events. Alluring Affairs was Janelle's heart and soul, as it gave her the opportunity to do what she did best—manage and plan. Her résumé of successful events spanned the globe, from corporate events for one of the world's largest banks to a stellar after-party during NYC's Fashion Week and the lavish wedding of their very own mayor.

Sandra's Swoon Couture was fast becoming one of the go-to boutiques for unique fashions. Her friend's focus was now on growing her business on a national level, which Janelle knew would be an absolute success, despite how Sandra's parents liked to downplay their daughter's dream.

As for Vicki, her passion had always been the whimsical beauty of floral design. Petals was the name of her flower shop that occupied the first floor of the grand yellow Victorian they'd transformed into their business offices.

"Girl, yes, I remember," Sandra replied. "Johnny Blackwell is all I have to say."

Janelle laughed and nodded. "Yes! You and Johnny Blackwell dancing so close Principal Chaney personally came to pry you two apart."

"And then you carried that X-rated mess back behind the bleachers, using me as a lookout. I should have made you pay me," Vicki added.

"Hmm, that seems like forever ago," Janelle stated. "Remember we were so ready to get out of this town and really live?" She definitely remembered that time herself, even if her best friends didn't. It had been a time of changes, of rejuvenation, of expectancy. Now, years later, Janelle felt more as if she was in a time of denial, or at least stagnation, and she wasn't quite sure how to deal with that revelation.

"What I remember are the nights we used to stay up late, drinking that nasty beer we'd snuck into the dorm," Vicki said. "We would lie on our beds, bottle in hand, and fantasize about our wedding day. Remember that?"

Janelle sat back in her chair. She remembered but for years had tried to forget. Not that the memory was painful; it was more that her perfect wedding would not come to fruition. The topic never failed to bring her spirits down, but as usual, she wouldn't let it show. Janelle Howerton would never taint her family's name with the darkness that had once hovered around her.

"I remember you talking about your dream wedding nonstop, like you thought Romeo was going to call to you from outside the window," Sandra added to Vicki with a chuckle.

"Don't laugh—I remember that perfectly, too." Vicki sat up straighter in her chair, her long hair pulled back into her signature tight bun, clearing her throat and smiling.

Janelle couldn't help but smile right along with her. Vicki had always been the romantic of the bunch. She was the one who maintained long-term monogamous relationships always with the hope of meeting Mr. Right, while over the years, Janelle and Sandra had resigned themselves to believe otherwise and to make the necessary concessions.

"Small, sweet and simple," Vicki continued. "That's what I want. I'll wear my mother's wedding dress and be surrounded by all my family and friends. It'll be perfect and romantic and everything I ever dreamed."

Sandra nodded. "And it will probably only happen in your dreams."

Janelle tried not to chuckle this time, noting the crestfallen look on Vicki's face at Sandra's words.

"It can happen for her," Janelle said, reaching a hand out to cover Vicki's. "If she believes in her heart that this is what's in store for her life, it can happen."

"Well," Sandra announced, slapping her palm on the table, "I believe that Swoon will become an international name among anyone looking for uniquely designed outfits. That's my goal for the foreseeable future—to hell with all this love and happily-ever-after."

"This coming from the woman who has had more dates than I can even imagine ever having in my entire life," Vicki responded.

Sandra shook her head, long highlighted strands of brown hair moving alongside her stylish hooped earrings. "A date is not a husband."

Janelle didn't speak but nodded her agreement. This was an old discussion that they'd had more times than she could count during their girls' meetings at the Quarterdeck. Since their return from college—and even though they worked in the same building and often collaborated throughout the day with each other—the ladies had had a standing ritual to meet every Monday at one of Wintersage's most popular taverns.

It helped that the Quarterdeck was located centrally, at the corner of Main Street, its back facing the bay with boats coming and going, right around the corner from the old Victorian they'd renovated for their offices.

While they normally chatted about business, the events they'd completed and the ones that were upcoming, the conversation, more often than not, ventured back to their own ideas about marriage and men, and so far nothing the others had to say was changing their viewpoints.

"Well, at least you're dating," Vicki continued, ducking her head as she twisted the stirrer in her white wine spritzer.

"Are you referring to me?" Janelle asked, knowing very well she was.

"There's only one of us here that hasn't had a man wine, dine and tap that behind in ages."

Sandra laughed at her own comment, while Vicki continued to avoid eye contact. These two had been in Janelle's life so long, they were the sisters she'd never had biologically, and they both meant well— she knew they did. But her reasons behind not dating and the strict guidelines she had for when she did date were her own business and she wasn't about to defend them. She couldn't.

"Whatever," she replied with a wave of her hand. "I'm not complaining."

And she wasn't. Her life was exactly the way she wanted it, her business was a success and she was healthy. What else could she ask for?

## Chapter 1

The minute he walked into the room, Janelle knew she was going to regret working from home this morning. But she'd awakened with a horrendous headache, the third one this week, and try as she might, the stress-free yoga DVD she'd purchased and the two ibuprofen she'd downed thirty seconds after rolling out of bed were not helping. The headache and tired shoulders and general feeling of fatigue were becoming an everyday occurrence for her and while she didn't want to become worried, she was.

Sitting at the dining room table with vendor contracts spread out in front of her, she looked up into the eyes of Darren Howerton Sr. and wanted to groan with annoyance. Sure, he was her father and there was no other man on this planet that she loved more, but his mere appearance in this room, at this time of day, meant he was about to ask her to do something. And from the way he pulled out the chair across from her with ever-so-slow movements before sitting and staring at her with almost apologetic eyes, she knew she was on point with her assessment.

"Hi, baby girl," he greeted her, smoothing his paisley-print tie down in front of him.

"Hi, Daddy," she replied expectantly.

"Are you busy? I need to talk to you."

While her father didn't openly suggest that Janelle's career as an event planner took a second seat to Howerton Computer Technologies, as Sandra's parents did with her career, his almost complete disregard of her career was a dead giveaway this was how he felt. So whenever he asked if she was busy, it really didn't matter if she said she was or not—he would proceed with whatever it was he wanted. She'd blame that on her mother if Susan Howerton hadn't died suddenly in a car accident five years ago. At any rate, Darren Howerton had gone from his own mother's overindulging arms straight into the arms of a young and eager-to-please wife, who made him feel as if he'd hung the stars and the moon. After her death, Darren expected Janelle to pick up the torch and treat him the same way. In addition to moving back to her childhood home to help her father cope, she'd slipped right into the pattern of expectancy her mother had created. She was basically there for whatever her father needed. Back then, it had been best for both of them. Janelle hadn't wanted to be alone—fear an all-

too-prevalent part of her life at that time. And her
father hadn't been able to be alone either; he would
surely have died of a broken heart if he had been.

"What can I do for you, Daddy?" she asked, attempting to let the past remain there.

"Ballard Dubois. Do you know who that is?"

Janelle figured she probably should, and maybe
if it hadn't felt as if someone were driving spikes
into her temples for the sheer hell of it, she could
have given it a little more thought. But things being
as they were, she didn't even try. "I don't think I do.
Why? Should I?"

Her father raised thick eyebrows, probably at the
spike in her tone, but he didn't speak of it, just continued on. She wasn't even surprised—her wants and
needs were always secondary.

"He runs Dubois Maritime Shipping with his father, Daniel. Hudson Dubois is the family patriarch,
the old coot. Each generation of Dubois is insanely
intelligent, shrewd and devoted to that company. But
Ballard's the one with his hand on the pulse of a growing political concern—health care."

Janelle watched as her father talked, engrossed by
the slightly raspy sound of his voice and the aristo-
cratic air he exuded when speaking about his business. What she couldn't figure out was where all this
business and political talk was going. Two years ago
her father had decided to hand over the reins of HCT
to Darren Jr., who was three years older than Janelle
and much more suited to work in the family business than she ever claimed to be. Not one to be idle,

Darren Sr. announced his candidacy for a seat in the state House of Representatives about six months ago.

With that flashback she thought of just how much she'd seen her father in the past six months. It hadn't been often since he'd completely thrown himself into the campaign. At any rate, she hadn't seen him this excited about anything since her mother's death. That was why she'd stopped what she was doing and tried like hell to ignore her headache to listen attentively to what he was saying. She owed him that much and probably ten times more after all she'd put him through when she ended her engagement with Jack.

"Health care is taking care of itself," she replied, "or rather, the current president is wading through those muddy waters."

"My platform needs a strong backing in this area," Darren continued as if she hadn't spoken at all. "Ballard, through his foreign and domestic dealings, has developed his own core of health-care reform supporters. Having Ballard and Dubois Maritime backing me would be beyond beneficial. It would give me the push I need to build an even bigger margin between myself and Oliver Windom."

In Janelle's estimation, Oliver Windom didn't stand a chance against the weight the Howerton name carried in Massachusetts. Still, she could tell her father felt very strongly about this. "Okay, I understand what you're saying. How will you go about getting them to back you?"

Darren smiled and Janelle almost faltered. It had been so long since she'd seen a genuine smile on her father's face. Sure, he'd appeared happy during the holidays and then at small family gatherings when Darren Jr.—DJ—had come into town. But for the most part, the day his wife died, the joy seemed to have died in him. Her heart ached at the thought.

"I'd like for you to schedule a meeting with Dubois. Visit him in his Boston office and talk to him about the campaign."

All other thoughts fled from Janelle's mind as she completely grasped what her father had been saying.

"You want *me* to get Ballard Dubois to support your campaign? Me? Not DJ?" she asked her father, more than a little amazed at what he was suggesting. It was obvious that since DJ had already taken over the family business, he was destined to follow in his father's footsteps, and as such would be the one building his family's legacy.

"DJ already has his hands full with the rollout for next year. Competition is fierce and HCT has to stay on top of the market."

She nodded, understanding what her father had just said, and the fact that he hadn't really answered her question.

"I have a business to run, too," she told him. "The mayor's executive assistant emails me at least four times a day about the homecoming dance and we have three more weddings before the end of this year." She was just as busy as DJ and she was certain that DJ hadn't been the one to swear off dating for fear of getting hurt and embarrassed the way she had been before. She was absolutely positive he wasn't the one who had almost been raped.

Darren leaned forward, his charcoal-gray suit jacket adjusting to the movement as he let his arms rest on the table, his gaze intent on his only daughter. "I need you to do this for me, Janelle. It's very important to the campaign."

*Say no. Say no. Scream the one-syllable word and then run like hell before he gets a chance to really work his persuasion skills.* It wasn't worth it; the risk far outweighed the gain. Didn't it?

"I don't have time to go to Boston right now, Daddy. I have vendors to interview, two site visits in as many days and a Skype conference with a French designer at the end of the week. I just can't," she told him, her heart pounding with the mere thought of going on this date, whatever the reason.

Darren shook his head. "You know, you look more like Susan every day," he began, his voice a little lower, his eyes… Were they blurring?

"Sometimes I hear you talking on the phone and I could swear it was her. I just listen and remember and miss her all over again."

She reminded him of her mother. Of course, she did look like Susan Howerton with her high cheekbones and eyes often called exotic due to their natural upward tilt. They also shared the same chocolate-brown complexion and wide smile. Janelle knew all this, had known it all her life. Still, when her father said it, when it caused him to miss her mother even more, she never knew what to say or how to handle it.

"You know she was the one to first talk about politics. She was sure it was the direction I needed to go in. It took me too long to realize she was telling the truth."

Janelle took a deep breath, listening to her father's deep and somehow desolate voice.

"I'll see if I can work a quick trip into my schedule, Daddy," she said, clenching her fingers as she did. "But I cannot make any promises."

Darren smiled. He stood then and came around the table. His hand was on hers as he leaned down closer, kissing her on the cheek. "You'll do wonderful, baby girl, just wonderful," he said before standing and leaving her alone once more.

When he was gone, the only thing that Janelle could recall about her father's presence was that he smelled like Calvin Klein Obsession cologne. That scent was just as dependable as her father had always been in her life. She'd always been able to count on him, always been able to run to him or her mother with whatever issues she had and know without a doubt they'd move mountains to fix them. Yet she hadn't come running home to them the night Jack had assaulted her. She hadn't run to anyone, for that matter. She'd handled the situation entirely on her own and she was still doing so. The only difference now was that she was tired of hauling guilt and fear around like carry-on luggage.

"I need your help, Janelle. I'm desperate," Rebecca Lockwood said from the other end of the phone. "I cannot bail on this client. Mal Harford is the owner of Pacific Royal Airlines. He's eccentric, to put it nicely, his wallet's bigger than his mouth, and what he wants he gets, all the time. Please say you'll do this for me."

Sitting in her office two days after the very strange conversation with her father, Janelle had thought she'd managed to escape drama for today. She had been wrong.

"Slow down. Wait a minute. What are you asking me to do exactly?" She really didn't want to do anything. Her workload was big enough and the Parents' Association was driving her absolutely insane over this homecoming. Clients that just signed checks and let her do her job were her favorite and she wished she had more of them.

Rebecca took a deep breath, let it out on a heavily exaggerated huff that made Janelle roll her eyes, then continued, "My younger sister Alexa just called to tell me she's having surgery on Friday morning. Her husband is serving his second tour in Iraq and she has a six-month-old daughter and nobody to help take care of either of them. So I have to leave for Colorado first thing tomorrow morning."

"Okay, sorry to hear that. Hope the surgery and the caretaking go well," Janelle replied with a nod, her attention traveling to the window, where she could see the sun finally beginning to set.

"Thanks," she said on another huff. "So what I'm asking you to do is supervise Harford's charity masquerade ball for me. This is a yearly event and I had to beat out six other bids to get the contract. It's Friday evening and all the vendors are in place. Everything is paid for and my staff will be on hand to assist. But this guy's one of my biggest clients this year and I'd like to have his return business. So I need somebody really fantastic to be here just in case something goes wrong."

Janelle didn't immediately respond.

"But nothing will go wrong," Rebecca continued. "I promise. There are just some really important people coming to this benefit and I want to make sure they have the best experience ever. But I have to be there for Alexa. So can you help? Please don't make me beg, Janelle," she finished finally.

Janelle couldn't help but smile. She'd known Rebecca for four years, since meeting her at an event-planning conference in Orlando. They'd kept in close contact since then, seeing each other at least twice a year at other industry events.

"You're talking about this Friday night? As in day after tomorrow?" she asked.

"Yes. I'm sorry for the short notice, but Alexa has to have this surgery sooner rather than later."

"I understand," Janelle said because she did. There was nothing she wouldn't do for Sandra or Vicki, who were the closest she would ever have to sisters. If they lived across the country and were having surgery, she'd be on a plane to them, as well.

"And all I have to do is supervise? Everything else is done?"

"Yes. I even called all the vendors to confirm this morning. I've briefed my staff and we did a last site visit at lunch today. So if you say yes, I can brief you on everything now and send you a complete copy of my file."

She couldn't say no. Janelle knew there was no good way to back out of this, and really, she didn't want to. For as busy as she was here in Wintersage, she felt as if getting out of town for a few days might be good. Things in the Howerton household had become quite tense with the election growing closer. Not to mention the fact that having a chance to work with Mal Harford—even secondhandedly—was a great coup for her career.

"I can give you thirty minutes to brief me. Then I need you to send me everything you have on Harford and this event. I'll make some adjustments and see when I can get up to Boston," Janelle told her.

Rebecca used one of those thirty minutes to thank Janelle and swear her debt and gratitude. Then they got down to business, which was a welcome distraction in Janelle's hectic life.

# Chapter 2

Ballard Dubois touched the edge of his plain black mask, lifting it slightly so that his vision would be unfettered. He hated attending these types of functions—not that he had anything against contributing to the research for and treatment of children with cancer, which was Mal Harford's favorite project since the death of his twin daughters when they were just ten years old. It was more that he didn't like the time it took away from working or thinking about how to move his family's company further into the twenty-first century. Still, public appearances had always been good for Dubois Maritime Shipping, a majority of their work connections having been made through the networking of his father and his grandfather before him. So getting out, being the face of the company, was a part of the job. If he thought of it that way, he could reconcile dressing in a tuxedo and even wearing this god-awful mask for the past hour and a half.

Harford's events always had a theme and this one was a masquerade. Ballard had to give it to the old man, he definitely knew how to draw rich and uptight socialites who were otherwise focused on making even more money than they already had out into a night of drinking and celebrating—and how to depart with some of their well-earned money. Tonight they were at Boston's Royale Nightclub, a different scene for this batch of upper-class characters but one of such creative allure, they couldn't resist the opportunity to attend.

The lighting and decor were phenomenal, gold, green and red illuminating the gleaming hardwood floors. Couches were strategically placed throughout the large space, while more than three hundred guests milled about sipping Perrier-Jouët, wearing formal attire and masks ranging from the ornate to the unembellished.

He'd been here for about an hour now, and he decided that thirty more minutes would meet his quota and he could head back to his penthouse. The evening had gone according to protocol as he'd spoken to two international vendors that worked with his company and had been introduced to, and had secured a private meeting with, Yujin Chan from the Chinese consulate in New York, whose family had a huge trade conglomerate and were currently looking for a U.S.

partner. So it had already been a good night as far as business was concerned.

And now, as he pulled his mask completely off and continued to stare at the tall, leggy beauty standing about ten feet away from him, it might just be heading in the same direction on a personal note.

She wore a black dress that scraped just past her knees in a fluid material that Ballard thought he just might be in love with. At her shoulders slips of that same material feathered over her skin. From the side, her curvaceous body was what had immediately caught his attention, plump backside and high palm-sized breasts that his palms actually itched to grip. Then she turned and his breath caught in his chest. He blinked just to make sure the lights weren't interfering with his vision. The dress that he was thanking the designer ten times over for creating took a deep plunge in the front, so deep he had to swallow twice, and even then his erection was still on the rise.

He took the first step toward her and realized music was playing, a mellow jazzy tune. Ballard didn't want to dance, but he did want her body close to his. Actually, he wanted her naked body on top of his naked body, but for now the dance would have to suffice. She turned again as someone came up behind her. They talked, and he watched her nodding slightly, hair pulled up high so that the length of her neck was bare. He barely registered the person beside her—if they were male or female or if they had horns or a floor-length tail. As he grew closer, another person approached her. It was a man, he noticed this time, and Ballard didn't like it.

The man said something and she extended her hand to him. "I'm Janelle Howerton. So nice to meet you, sir," she replied.

*Janelle Howerton.* The name seemed familiar but not really, as though maybe he'd heard it over the course of the past few weeks. Then again, he'd heard a barrage of names, since their annual meeting of the board was a month ago in New York City, where their newest warehouse had just been expanded. He might have heard the name there but he wasn't sure. And right now he didn't really give a damn. All that mattered was that he was now close enough to get a serious whiff of her perfume and his body heated instantly.

"Would you like to dance?" Ballard found himself asking even though he distinctly remembered not wanting to dance a few minutes ago.

She turned to face him then, and only because he was a thirty-five-year-old man, with vast experience when it came to the opposite sex and the responsibility of running a multibillion-dollar company on his shoulders, did he not gawk at her striking beauty and fall at her feet.

"Ah, I don't think so," she said, the soft lilt of her voice as alluring as the smooth milky complexion of her skin.

"Sure, go ahead. I won't hold you up," the man who had been talking to her said. He even extended a hand to touch her elbow—which irritated Ballard to no end—edging her closer to him. "You two young people go ahead and cut a rug. Shame to put this great band to waste," the man continued.

"Thank you, sir. Shall we?" Ballard extended his hand to her, almost couldn't wait for the moment she put her palm in his, and attempted a smile.

They'd barely moved three feet before he turned and pulled her slowly into his arms, letting the music wash through his mind and guide his movements instead of giving his body full control—his body, which was already in overdrive from the quick and potent attraction to this woman.

"Well," she said once her hands settled on his shoulders, "I hope you're enjoying yourself tonight."

"I am now," was his quick response. "How about you?"

She shrugged. "I'm actually working, but this is a really nice event."

"Working?"

"Yes, I'm managing the event tonight. So I probably shouldn't continue dancing."

"But we're so good at it," he replied, pulling her just a bit closer. She felt soft and pliant in his arms, his hand resting at the small of her back, his gaze focused on her face, partially covered by the black domino mask. It had an intricate design that laced around each of her eyes, coming to sexy points at her temples, decorated with white rhinestones. Another rhinestone twinkled over the bridge of her nose and he found himself wanting to touch it, to rub his fingers along the mask, then remove it to see the complete beauty of her face.

He cleared his throat, determined to act like a normal, functioning human and not the bundle of hormones he actually felt like instead. "So you work for the club?"

"Oh, no. The event planners," was her response.

She looked around the room then and he figured, with the job she'd just told him about, she was checking to see if all was going well.

"It's a great event. I'm sure Harford will receive a ton of hefty donations."

This time she nodded, her gaze returning to him. Her eyes were brown with tiny flecks of gold, or maybe that was the lighting again. Either way, he liked them.

"That's wonderful. It's such a good cause. My father donates."

"Yes, a wonderful cause indeed." He was about to say something else but she'd mentioned her father and then the name clicked in his head. "Is your father Darren Howerton?"

She stopped dancing, looking at him with perplexity. "Ah, yes, he is. Do you know him?"

He nodded, letting the weight of the situation rest slowly in his mind. "I've never met him personally, but my family knows of him, of his campaign, I should say."

"Oh, really?" Her voice seemed just a little brighter. "I guess we should have taken care of these formalities already, but I'm Janelle Howerton."

Ballard smiled, as he already knew that. "And I'm Ballard Dubois."

His smile wavered only because hers did, the cordial and sexually charged air around them dissipating with the motion.

"You're Ballard Dubois?" she asked.

"Yes. Is that a problem?"

Slowly, prettily, her smile slipped back into place but didn't quite elicit that sparkle he'd previously seen in her eyes. "Not a problem, just a coincidence."

"Well, I don't really believe in coincidences. I do, however, believe in chance and I would be terribly remiss if I didn't take this chance to invite you to dinner with me tomorrow night."

She hesitated, looking around the room again. They'd resumed dancing but now she stopped again, taking a step back so that their bodies were no longer touching. He missed her instantly.

"That sounds nice," she replied, her tone a little more standoffish than it had been before. "I'm staying at the Four Seasons. But I should really get back to work."

Ballard would accept that excuse, for now. He reached for her hand and lifted it to his lips, kissed the back as his gaze remained focused on her. "I'll pick you up tomorrow at seven."

She smiled again, a wide brilliant smile that might have been practiced but rubbed along his body like warm oil anyway. "I'll see you tomorrow at seven," she said before slipping her hand from his and turning to walk away.

Ballard watched her walk. He watched the sway of her ass, the line of her shoulders, the curve of her calves, and he wanted her. Damn but he wanted her like he'd never wanted another woman in his life.

In his king-size bed hours later, Ballard lay on his back, his eyes closed but still seeing her, her scent still wafting through the air around him.

This was ridiculous. He did not do this over women. Ever. He met them, conversed with them, took them out, slept with them and then moved on. The connections were mutually beneficial in the physical sense and usually unsatisfactory on any long-term platform. He'd gone through his entire adult life perfecting that situation; until now he barely remembered most of the women who had been in his life.

Yet he remembered Janelle Howerton with startling clarity.

In fact, he thought, his hand drifting down beneath the sheet, the hot weight of his length waiting, he remembered too much about her. Like the softness of her skin, which Ballard believed would most likely encompass the entire stretch of her body. The graceful curves of her breasts and backside that had his length jutting upward.

When his fingers wrapped around his erection, prepared to go along with the memory and take him to a pleasurable release, he moaned. Then he yanked his hand from beneath the blanket, thoroughly agitated with himself for even thinking about going there.

That wasn't the type of man he was. He didn't need

to pleasure himself when there were so many other women out there who were up to the task.

But his dreams didn't continue with any of those other women; they progressed with one female in particular as the star performer. Cloaked only in the intriguing black domino mask, she enticed him throughout his sleep, pushing him to the brink until the next moment he woke in a sweat, erection so hard it was painful, mind so full of her he almost whispered her name—Janelle.

# Chapter 3

He was not what she'd expected.

Actually, Janelle hadn't expected anything where Ballard Dubois was concerned, because he'd been the absolute last person on her mind. The man her father asked her to speak with, to convince to support his campaign, had not been on her radar at all. Last night had been all about making Mr. Harford's party a success for Rebecca's sake as well as for her own. Now that it seemed she'd done that—as evidenced by Mr. Harford's continual praise throughout the event and once he and his wife were preparing to leave—Janelle could allow herself to think about that other matter.

He was tall and extremely good-looking, two things she hadn't really considered he might be after her conversation with her father. He smelled good, which was always a huge plus in Janelle's book. Dancing was definitely something he did well, in addition to holding a female close enough to make her almost swoon—which hadn't happened to her in more years than she could count.

Swooning meant falling and falling meant giving up every piece of who she was to someone who might or might not handle that commodity with care. Giving up everything left one extremely vulnerable and susceptible to deceit and, later, absolute mortification. In essence, to Janelle's way of thinking, and courtesy of her past relationship, swooning was the beginning of the end. It was a definite no-no, as evidenced by her lack of dating life and the intention to keep that plan going.

With that said, Ballard Dubois and his lean build, pecan skin tone, close-cropped black hair and neatly barbered goatee could certainly make a woman want to change her mind about the no-dating status. A woman other than Janelle.

Yet here she was, preparing for a dinner date with him. No, correction, this was not a date, because Janelle did not date. She was meeting with him as a favor to her father and that was all. The butterflies flitting around in the pit of her stomach as she rode the elevator down to the lobby told another story entirely, but she'd decided to ignore them no matter how persistent they seemed.

She'd dressed in a simple pantsuit, one of two she'd brought with her just in case, navy blue with a short jacket and a silver shell beneath. Her shoes were new, four-inch-heel pewter platforms that she loved like the French toast she'd had for breakfast. Her hair was down, straight and pulled over her left shoulder—the down-and-casual look. One hour was all she'd allotted for this little get-together. Then she was hitting the road, heading back to Wintersage and the many meetings she'd had to reschedule with the Parents' Association and other vendors to discuss the infamous homecoming dance.

Traffic in the lobby was pretty busy and Janelle found herself looking from the front entrance to the walkway, both viable spots for Mr. Dubois to enter the lobby. A glance at her watch confirmed he was late, by four minutes exactly. She was a stickler for being prompt, early if possible, hating the notion of abusing anyone's time. Clearly, he did not subscribe to the same belief.

She folded her arms, gazing down at the bold black-and-gold floor design, then up to the vibrant and colorful floral arrangements strategically placed around the area. Vicki would love the color selection and how it offset the dark flooring. She probably would have stood here rearranging the position of the flowers to her liking for a better vantage point, or most certainly would have examined them for the best use of color and variety. Vicki was a perfectionist that way, Janelle thought with an inner smile. Janelle, Vicki and Sandra were all similar in that regard. That was why the Silk Sisters had garnered such rave reviews for their work.

"I hope that smile on your face is because you're thinking of me."

His smooth, deep voice interrupted her thoughts and Janelle tried not to be annoyed by that fact coupled with his tardiness. She also tried not to notice how good he looked in his smoke-gray suit with the faintest pinstripe and ice-blue dress shirt and matching tie. There was no doubt that a man who could wear a suit well was tops in her book, but there was also no doubt that she was not supposed to look at Ballard Dubois that way.

"Actually, no, but that doesn't mean that I'm not pleased to see you," was her cordial reply.

"Okay, well, we'll let my bruised ego deal with that later," he said, offering his arm to her. "Shall we?"

It was a little much, she thought. She didn't need to walk arm in arm with him to have dinner. Still, she reminded herself that she was doing this for her father, for his precious campaign, as she laced her arm through Ballard's and walked with him toward the hotel's very popular lounge.

"I figured you would be tired from last night's festivities and made reservations someplace close," he told her as they moved through the glass-door entrance.

Great, she thought, giving him a nod and smile of agreement. She wouldn't have far to go to get back to her room.

Once they were seated, Janelle allowed herself another indulgent look at her dinner partner. Damn, that suit looked good on him, or was it that the man might possibly look good in anything? She wasn't sure. A gold watch—she didn't even guess at the name brand, knowing instinctively it would be expensive—glimmered at his right wrist, a huge signet ring casting the same posh glow on his right ring finger.

"So, your family has made quite a name for itself in the shipping industry. I've heard nothing but glowing remarks about Dubois Maritime."

"Really? Do you work with a lot of clients in the shipping industry?" he asked in what sounded to Janelle like a skeptical tone.

"As a matter of fact, I was born and raised in Wintersage. Our founding fathers made their fortune in the shipping industry. My family's very active throughout the town, so hearing your company's name mentioned from time to time isn't all that unusual."

*So there,* she thought, lifting the glass of water the waitress had discreetly placed in front of her for a sip.

"Wintersage," he repeated thoughtfully. "That's about an hour or so away from Boston, correct?"

"Correct," she replied even though she got the impression he knew exactly where Wintersage was. He'd probably done precisely what she had this morning and researched everything about her family on the internet. She was not fooled by his very calm, very assessing demeanor, not one bit—especially considering how scrumptious he looked wearing that demeanor.

Wow, she really needed to calm her raging and self-deprived hormones.

"So you're heading the company now. That's a huge responsibility for someone so young. Has it been difficult for you?" she asked.

He smiled then, slow, knowing, and she shifted a bit in her chair, covering the action by picking up the menu and acting as if that held more of her interest.

"One misstep will not end the date, Janelle," he commented.

Her head immediately snapped up. "This is not a date," she stated firmly. "And what misstep?"

His smile stayed in place, the expression a bit on the arrogant side, but she was trying to make this work, for her father's sake.

"I'm not running the company just yet. My grandfather is still the CEO, my father the CFO. Right now I'm the regional manager, so I handle all of the day-to-day operations."

He spoke as if he were educating her and Janelle was immediately offended. She had already opened her mouth to fire back when he held up a hand to stop her.

"I'm joking," he said, chuckling lightly afterward.

Her lips snapped closed and she sat back in her chair, eyeing him suspiciously.

"You looked like you were ready to give me hell, so I figured I'd better clear that up quickly," he continued.

Janelle had to smile in response. "Not quite hell, but I was going to say a few things."

He nodded, his laughter subsiding. "I know it. But I'd like for us to have a nice dinner, to get to know each other better. So if it makes you feel better, we won't call this a date. Besides, it's probably better that way."

Now she was offended again, or at least she thought she should be. But maybe not, since she'd been telling herself all day long that this wasn't a date. She admitted only to herself that for the first time in a very long time, she was thrown off—even marginally—by a man.

"I would like to have a nice dinner, as well. So I won't ask why it's better not to call this a date."

But she just had, hadn't she? Maybe she should just leave.

"When I date a female, we focus on getting to know each other, and if that's pleasing to us both, we take it to the next level," he stated as if he were reading a report at a meeting.

"The next level being sex?" she asked without her normal processing-before-speaking rule.

He lifted a hand and smoothed down his tie, the motion confident, probably overly so, but intriguing at the same time. If she had to sum up Ballard Dubois right at this moment, she'd peg him as a conceited, self-important businessman who was used to getting exactly what he wanted. Which to her and for the purpose she was here for tonight was going to mean she had her work cut out for her, and she wasn't certain she wanted to go that route just to get his family's support.

"Yes, the next level being sex," he answered.

"So you have a very methodical way of dating, I

see." Whereas she had a method of her own—don't do it!

"I like to look at it as logical structuring," was his reply. He leaned forward, pushing his menu to the side, his dreamy brown eyes holding her gaze captive. "It is logical to date before sleeping with someone because it clarifies the understanding between the two adults before their focus shifts to more physical pleasures. Once that understanding is perfectly clear, future dealings are smoother."

"And by *future dealings* you mean for the time you wish to continue sleeping with her. What happens when that time is up?" she asked, curious and simultaneously annoyed at his candid nonchalance when it came to dating and relationships.

"You're angry," he said with a nod. "Let's change the subject, since this is not a date."

Janelle did not want to change the subject. She wanted to leave. She wanted to get as far away from this infuriating, egotistical man as she could. But if she didn't get this out of the way now, she'd have another bullheaded man to deal with and she really wasn't up for that battle either. So she stayed for dinner, ate her food, participated in the basic conversation and counted the minutes until she could slip that key card into the door of her room and get the hell away from Ballard Dubois!

Ballard had insisted on walking her to her door. He knew that their evening had started out strenuous but was pleased that eventually, it had warmed into a pleasant experience. He'd asked her about her business, which calmed and animated her. The way in which she spoke about her events was both passionate and professional and he found himself wanting to have some type of party or gathering just to have the chance to be around her again.

At one point she'd shared a story about a client who had endured one disastrous wedding planner after another until finally contracting with her Alluring Affairs. She'd laughed and he'd felt as if he'd been punched in the chest, the air so swiftly leaving him at the sound.

A strong physical reaction, he'd realized, and had proceeded with the evening, not giving it much more thought.

Now, standing in front of her with her back to the door of her room, he couldn't help but think of the way he'd felt in the restaurant, because he was feeling the same way now. Seeing her face unobscured by a mask tonight had been a huge plus, but then, he'd already known she was a very attractive woman. The slight upward slant of her eyes, her full lips and the smooth milk-chocolate tone of her skin had blood rushing quickly through his veins.

"Ballard?"

He blinked as he heard his name on her lips, recovering quickly from his momentary speechlessness as he stared at her.

"A good-night kiss," he whispered, moving in closer.

Her open palms immediately came to his chest,

pushing slightly against him, to stop him, Ballard was certain. The problem with that motion was that it hadn't reached her eyes. Instead, as Ballard looked at Janelle, he saw her lips parting slightly, her tongue snaking out to lick the bottom one, then retreating inside quickly as she cleared her throat.

"Yes," he began, reaching a hand up to rub the back of his fingers along her cheekbone down to the line of her jaw. "You can agree because you want to. Or you can simply tell me no and I'll leave."

She hesitated, her hands still on his chest, burning the desire he was already ensconced in deeper into his soul. After another second or so of indecision her lips parted once more, a small sound escaping.

"Ye—" she began to say.

And Ballard moved in, swooping his lips down over hers, taking the plumpness into his mouth for a deep suckle before pressing his tongue inside.

She replied hungrily, grabbing the lapels of his jacket tightly in her fingers, tilting her head slightly so that when he deepened the kiss, she was more than ready. On the inside, Ballard quivered, his entire body vibrating in reaction to her proximity, her scent, her taste. His hands cupped her face, slipping back until his fingers were tangled in the thick mass of her hair, holding her head steadily where he wanted it, where he could plunder her mouth mercilessly.

He pressed her into the door, his body flush against hers, his rigid erection most likely felt by her as he did. The fact that they were in a hotel hallway, that at any moment someone could come out of another room or off the elevator and see them, lingered somewhere in the back of his mind. Alongside was the fact that they'd gone to great lengths to clarify that this was not a date, and if it had been, it was still too soon for a reaction such as this, a joining of passion like this. But he couldn't stop, wouldn't even consider pulling his lips, his hands, his body away from hers at this moment. It felt too good, felt…almost…right.

It was Janelle who made the move to break away. Simultaneously releasing his jacket and turning her head away from him, she gasped once for breath before saying in a very quiet voice, "Good night, Ballard."

He released her then. Of course, he had no idea how when his body was sending every sign possible indicating it wanted to stay precisely where it was. Still, he took the necessary steps backward, even cleared his throat to let her know he was still standing there since she wouldn't look at him.

"Good night, Janelle," he said, and forced himself to walk away.

This was not the norm for either of them, Ballard suspected, but most assuredly not for him. He needed time to breathe some fresh air, to clear his mind, to let this raging erection subside and to figure out just what he planned to do next where Janelle Howerton was concerned.

# Chapter 4

She'd spent the morning returning phone calls from vendors—the caterer was locked in, the stellar menu including a great grilled Maine lobster with chive risotta that Janelle had been privy to tasting a week ago. Vicki was contracted for the floral arrangements; Janelle knew she didn't need to do more than send Vicki an email with the date, time and colors, and everything would be taken care of from there.

That was the type of rhythm their friendship had. Whenever she booked a wedding, she referred the bridal party to Sandra for their wardrobe and to Vicki for the flowers. Likewise, her friends referred their clients to her for all their event-planning needs. They were a solid unit, just as Janelle thought a couple should be, complementing each other in business and on a personal level.

Something she and Ballard Dubois did not do.

And why she was even thinking about Ballard for the billionth time today, she had no idea. When she'd arrived home after her dinner with Ballard, her father had already been gone. She'd written him a short note saying she'd met and had dinner with Ballard but that they hadn't had the opportunity to really get into the political discussion. She strategically left out that it had been because they'd been too busy talking about her job and his to get around to speaking about whether he and his company would back her father's campaign. Darren would bring that up the first chance he got, so she made a note to be prepared for that conversation.

Ballard was an extremely proud man who took running his family business very seriously. He didn't strike her as the kind of man who was simply along for the ride, taking what was given to him. No, he clearly worked very hard for the company, his vision for expansion that he'd shared with her seeming very promising. So much so she'd found herself offering to help him announce the new locations via a spectacular opening event. Surprisingly, he'd been very agreeable to that suggestion.

Dinner had turned out well, considering how it had begun. And the good-night kiss. Damn. That was all she could think of to describe it.

Janelle's fingers froze over her keyboard with that thought. She'd been typing budget figures into her accounting database but now couldn't do anything but remember last night.

That kiss.

It had been just…so…*damn,* again.

With a sigh, Janelle sat back in her chair, turning so that she was now facing the window. It was nearing six o'clock in the evening, so some of the local fishermen were pulling into dock with the second part of their haul for the day. Over the next few months traffic at the dock would slow to almost nonexistence as the winter chill settled over their little shipping town. Farther up the road, she could see more houses like the one they'd renovated that also sheltered local businesses. Most of them would be closing up for the winter. The fresh seafood market was one. Another was the gift shop that specialized in Wintersage trinkets handmade by Selia DuVane, an eighty-something-year-old lifelong town resident who used the colder months and lack of tourists to replenish her stock.

Black lampposts occupying each corner were now draped in orange-and-brown ribbons signifying the imminent arrival of fall, at which time the town wholeheartedly adopted the harvest decor. Staring out at the traditional, the safe and steady she knew she could rely on, calmed Janelle. Whereas each time her thoughts drifted to Ballard Dubois, which had been too many times to count, her heart rate increased, worry tapping an annoying rhythm against her temples.

"Whoa, she's in deep thought. Maybe we should go."

She heard Vicki's voice from behind and turned in her chair.

"Please, that's the best time to sit down and find out what's on her mind," Sandra quipped, already entering Janelle's office and taking a seat in one of the honey-colored guest chairs that complemented her light oak desk and the warm beige-painted walls.

"Nothing's on my mind but work," Janelle told them with a sigh of resignation. The numbers she was crunching would have to wait a little longer.

Vicki had followed Sandra's lead, taking a seat in the matching guest chair. This was after she'd glanced at Sandra, then at Janelle. Something was going on.

"What's up with you two?"

Sandra shook her head. "Not a chance," she said, waving a finger, one long fuchsia-painted nail in front of her. "You've been closed in this office all day either on the phone or staring at that computer. Now, I know we're all busy but we never forget Monday nights. Never," she reiterated.

Janelle sat back in her chair, clasping her fingers together as she looked at her friends. A part of her wanted to curse the fact that she had completely forgotten about their weekly meeting. Another part wanted to moan, because she could use a drink right now.

"I'm sorry—I had a lot of catching up to do since I took those days to go up to Boston and take care of the party for Rebecca. I just got caught up. We can go now if you want."

Sandra shook her head once more. "Or we can sit right here while you tell us what's going on."

"She doesn't have to tell us, Sandra," Vicki chimed in. "We know what's bothering her. The same thing that's been on all of our minds today. We might as well get it out in the open."

Janelle couldn't help but feel a bit confused, even though she'd figured there was something wrong, with the way they'd both come in here. "What's been on our minds, Vicki?"

Sandra rolled her eyes, picking at nonexistent lint on her skirt. "It's not a big deal. Vicki's just being melodramatic, as she's been known to be before."

Vicki frowned. "No. I'm being realistic and I'm sharing my feelings with my two closest friends. That is what friends do, isn't it?" she proposed, arching an eyebrow at Sandra, who refused to look at her.

"Okay, you two, what is it?" Janelle finally asked.

"My brother took a job working on Oliver Windom's campaign. Vicki thinks it's a big deal. She thinks this election business might get weird for us, working together and being friends," Sandra said in what sounded like one breath.

"That's not what I said," Vicki told Sandra, then looked at Janelle. "I was just concerned about us having to choose sides. We've been friends forever. Now your father is running for the House of Representatives and Sandra's brother is working for his biggest opponent. That's a huge conflict."

Great, the election again. Janelle was officially tired of the pending election and it was still weeks

away. Sure, she was proud of her father, always had
been, but she just did not need this added drama in
her life. Having dinner with a guy that she normally
would stay a couple of states away from and now
watching one of her friends stress over something
that shouldn't be an issue for either of them. Still,
with a deep inhale and slow exhale, she understood
where Vicki was coming from. She also knew that
all her frustration was not coming from this election.

"There's no conflict for me," she told them. "This
is a free country—vote for who you want. All I ask
is that you remain informed while doing so."

Sandra laughed. "Exactly. Do what you want.
Hasn't that always been our motto?"

Vicki smiled. "Yes, it has. But you sound like an
infomercial," she told Janelle.

"What? Why? I'm just saying that there are two
things never to be discussed at work—politics and
religion. Freedom to worship who or what you want
as well as to go to the polls and put in your ballot."

"And you don't care if we don't vote for your dad?"
Vicki persisted.

Without thinking—actually, sick and tired of having *been* thinking on one particular subject all day—
Janelle let her head fall back on her chair. She closed
her eyes, bringing her fingers up to massage her temples. "Girl, please, I am so sick of thinking about my
father's campaign and what he needs to win this election. I don't know why it's my job to secure this last
bit of support for him. Why'd I have to go out with
the stuffy, arrogant man just to get his vote? Damn."

The second the diatribe was complete, Janelle recognized her mistake. Her head jerked up to both ladies staring at her, Sandra with an elegantly arched eyebrow lifted in question, Vicki with her mouth gaped open.

"You went out with a man?" Sandra asked slowly.

Vicki held up a finger. "Correction—a stuffy, arrogant man."

Janelle sighed. "Damn. Again," she muttered. "I can already see we're not going to leave this building without me telling you this, so here it goes. And before I start, it's nothing. Absolutely nothing. Understand?"

Sandra and Vicki shared a conspiratorial look, then turned their full attention back to her.

"His name is Ballard Dubois. My father wants his family's support for the campaign. He asked me to go out with him to gain that support. I wasn't going to, or rather, I didn't want to but I felt trapped. You know how my father is," she said, letting out another sigh, then looking down at her own neatly manicured nails. She hated how compelled she felt to please her father, to make up for the embarrassment she and her failed attempt at marriage had caused years ago.

"Anyway, I did that party for Rebecca over the weekend and just my luck, Ballard Dubois was in attendance," she continued, refusing to reflect on the past another second of this day.

"Okay, just for clarification," Sandra said, leaning forward, her legs crossed, "you are talking about *the* Ballard Dubois. *Forbes* Top Ten Richest Men Under

Forty for the last six years. He was on the cover of *GQ* just a few months ago with those sexy-ass eyes and was reported to be involved with Alaya Bentley, the next Diahann Carroll of the movie screen."

Of course that was the Ballard Dubois she was speaking of, and all that irrelevant information Sandra had just offered, Janelle had learned just this morning when she'd continued looking into his life via Google.

"*That* Ballard Dubois?" Vicki echoed the query.

Janelle tried to reroute their thoughts, and her own, for that matter. "Ballard Dubois who is next in line to take over Dubois Maritime Shipping, the successful businessman with enough power and influence to bring my father the final votes he needs to clinch this election. That's the one I'm referring to."

"Mmm-hmm." Sandra sat back in her chair. "Continue."

They were thinking something, Janelle could tell, and whatever it was, she didn't want to hear it. She just did not want to go there.

"So anyway, we end up dancing together. I didn't know who he was and he didn't know who I was until the end of the dance. Then he asked me to dinner and I agreed because of my father's request. I figured since fate was lending a hand, I'd just get the deed over with. We went to dinner last night and now I'm home. Deal done."

There was silence as she finished speaking, silence and staring. Janelle was on the receiving end of those knowledgeable stares that only people who knew things like when she'd had her first period, her first kiss, her first sexual experience, could dish out. In essence, they knew all her firsts, which meant they probably knew her as well as she knew herself. *Damn* was beginning to be the theme of the day for her.

"And which deal would that be? Hot sweaty sex with that fine-ass, rich-ass man?"

Leave it to Sandra to keep things in perspective. Janelle waited, knowing instinctively that Vicki would follow up. See, she knew her friends just as well as they knew her.

"Or did you get the support your father needed?" Vicki asked—as expected.

"Hell, if she went for the hot, sweaty sex, then that instantly sealed the political deal. Please, tell me I'm right," Sandra implored with her signature smile. The one that made you believe you could do whatever it was she was so excited about and at the same time made men want to fall at her feet.

Janelle simply shook her head. "There was no sex and we didn't talk enough about politics for me to secure his support."

Vicki looked confused "So you just ate? No talking, no nothing."

"We talked," Janelle replied simply. "We talked about my job and about his job. About his take on dating and how absurd I thought it was."

Sandra interrupted quickly. "You mean to tell me someone else has a dating criteria like you and you disagreed with him?"

"First, I do not have a criteria. I just choose not to

date. Second, he has this system—first date, discussion about where this could lead, when they'll have sex, when it will end. Nonsense like that is what I disagree with."

"That's not necessarily a bad thing," Vicki offered. "You could think of it as having a business plan, which we all do."

"Plenty of people have made sex a viable business," Sandra began, holding up a hand to stop Janelle's instant protest. "But not you, and I don't think Dubois either. The problem may be that both of you are overthinking this. Just go with the flow. Sleep together if you want. Move on if you have to," she finished.

"You sound like those girls we talked about back in college," Janelle added with a grin of her own. The Silk Sisters had always been the most sought-after females in school, the prettiest, most times the richest and the majority of the time the most difficult to attain. That had been their reputation and now, looking at them as adults, they seemed to be in the same boat. Janelle wondered why that thought made her worry.

"I'm not saying you should pick up your tramp card and hit the streets," Sandra corrected. "But, Janelle, it's been five years since that mess with Jack. That's five years since we all discovered he was an asshole. Not just you and not by yourself. We were there, remember."

Oh, how she remembered. Janelle sat back again, looking out the window this time. She didn't want to think about Jack Trellier or their wedding that never happened, didn't want to think about how embarrassed and betrayed she'd felt that day and the hundreds of days to follow. And she definitely did not want to think about the secret she still kept from her best friends.

"I agree," Vicki said. "It's time to move on."

Janelle almost said she had moved on. She almost argued that they were completely off base and that her reservations about dating, casual or otherwise, were not rooted in the broken heart her former fiancé had handed to her on a silver platter and the shame he'd served her as dessert. But these were her friends, and if she could limit her dishonesty with them, then she would.

"This is a business deal for my father. It's not personal," she reminded them when she looked their way again.

"Did you talk about politics at all during dinner?" Sandra asked.

"No," Janelle replied.

"Did he kiss you good-night?" was Vicki's question.

Janelle sighed again, the memory bringing a soft smile to her lips. "It was one hell of a good-night kiss, too."

Sandra was instantly smiling. "Then that means the hot steamy sex is imminent. Let's get to the Quarterdeck, order our drinks and discuss what you should wear for this night of seduction."

Vicki stood, joining Sandra on their way out the door.

"Ah, we don't have another date scheduled. I mean, he lives in Boston and I'm here and I was just going to send him an email asking about my father's campaign, then maybe follow that with a call in a week or so. That's all," she told them frankly.

It was Vicki this time who walked over to Janelle's desk and tapped her finger on the phone. "Call him."

"What? I can't—"

Vicki shook her head. That tight bun she kept in her hair always made her look more serious, more reserved than she actually was. Sandra had been after her for years to update her style a little more. It had been unsuccessful and they often joked about it, but this was the Vicki Janelle knew and loved, so it didn't matter much to her.

"You are a strong, confident, independent, successful black woman. There's nothing wrong with you asking a man out if you're interested in him," she told her.

Sandra spoke up then. "I agree. We'll give you ten minutes to make the call, schedule a date and meet us downstairs at the door."

Within the next minute, they were gone and Janelle was once again alone at her desk, staring at the phone, at the exact spot Vicki's finger had tapped. After a few stilted seconds, she looked at her computer monitor, minimizing the screen with her budget information to view the screen she'd spent way too much time browsing today—the Dubois Maritime Shipping website. She scrolled down until she found the Boston office number, then paused once more, looking at the phone, then back at the screen.

Finally, with an exaggerated exhale, she mumbled, "What the hell?" and picked up the phone to begin dialing.

The palatial estate located in the Weston area of Boston where Hudson, the creator of Dubois Maritime Shipping and the irrefutable patriarch of the Dubois family, and Leandra Dubois had raised their only son, Daniel, was full of love and laughter tonight. One day out of every month, Ballard and his father, Daniel, had dinner with Ballard's grandparents.

Sitting at the end of the eight-foot-long cross-banded double-pedestal mahogany table was Hudson, at eighty-five years old still smiling and laughing jovially as he shared his most recent antics on the golf course.

"I don't know why he keeps going out there when he knows he can't play," Leandra, Hudson's wife of sixty-three years, looked to her left, smiling lovingly at her husband.

"Never give up," Hudson declared. "That's the Dubois mantra. Never give up, no matter what."

"Even if the outcome will most likely remain the same," Daniel Dubois, solemn and often-contentious only son, replied to his father.

"Man can never know the outcome," Hudson replied stoically, glancing at Daniel.

Ballard lifted his glass to his lips, remaining silent in the midst of an old feud between his father and grandfather. The day after Ballard's high school graduation his mother, Gina Dubois, sat him down and told him she was leaving the stately home they shared with his father.

"I don't love him anymore and he's never known how to love me," Gina had told her only child.

Ballard hadn't completely understood what that meant and had figured at the time that it didn't really matter. His parents were getting divorced and he was thankfully going away to college. Hudson believed that Daniel should have fought harder for his marriage, that he should have made whatever concessions he could to keep Gina in his life. Daniel disagreed, believing instead that every person had her own path to walk and that if Gina's was taking her in a different direction, then so be it. He'd let his wife go and delved even deeper into the business that had been hugely responsible for the breakup in the first place. After graduating from Duke, Ballard had followed in his father's footsteps, spending the bulk of his days either in the office or on the road doing business for the company. That was his path and he was content with it because he didn't have a family of his own that he was responsible for.

"I met Darren Howerton's daughter the other night," Ballard said in an effort to cut through the tension that threatened to choke everyone in this room.

"Of Howerton Technologies?" his father inquired.

"His son's running the company now. Howerton's running for the House of Representatives seat that Edgar Mann is vacating," Ballard replied.

Daniel nodded. "Yes, I remember reading that a few months back. He was speaking at a fund-raiser when I was in Dallas. We had planned to meet up but never did."

"Howerton," Hudson was saying. "He's from around here, isn't he?"

"Wintersage," Ballard offered. "The family has been there since the town was founded."

Daniel finished chewing and taking a drink from his wineglass. He was wiping his hands on a napkin when he offered, "They have big ties in technology, Dad, so you probably wouldn't know much about them."

Hudson frowned. "When I started my company, I made it my business to know about locally influential African-Americans. I remember the Howerton name because of that town they're in. Shipping's always been big there."

Ballard nodded. "That's the same thing Janelle said."

"Janelle?" Leandra inquired, her eyebrows arching with interest. "Who is Janelle, dear?"

Despite all his travels, which had put him in the company of princesses from distant islands, movie stars and supermodels, his grandmother was still the most beautiful woman Ballard had ever seen. Even with her headful of silver-gray hair, her light brown eyes still held a twinkle of life he'd yet to glimpse in any other female. He loved her beyond words. And he knew her mind was perking right up at his mentioning a woman's name at the dinner table.

Normally, Ballard made it a point to keep his family and his personal dalliances separate. It was cleaner that way, more efficient and admittedly less stressful. He wondered why he hadn't thought of that before mentioning Janelle.

"She's Darren Howerton's daughter. I met her at Harford's fund-raiser over the weekend. We went to dinner Saturday night."

There, that should be enough to keep his grandmother smiling for days to come.

"I thought you sent me a text that you were meeting with Chan on Saturday evening," Daniel stated.

"I rescheduled," he replied.

"We need that deal to go through, Ballard. Handling all the freight from China to the States would be a phenomenal coup for us," his father continued.

"Tell me more about this Janelle Howerton. What does she do?" Hudson interjected.

While Ballard did not want to encourage anything where his grandparents were concerned, he also did not want to go back and forth with his father. Daniel was of the belief that Ballard still needed his father to tell him how to do his job. He didn't. He'd been handling Dubois business for more than ten years now, had taken the company further into the digital age than his father had ever dreamed. Chan and his business would still be there the middle of this week, when he'd rescheduled the meeting. And Ballard would clinch that deal, there was no doubt. So there was nothing left to discuss with his father.

"She's an event planner running her own company

in Wintersage. Very intelligent woman," he added but wasn't quite sure why.

His father made some sound that indicated he was not at all thrilled with the line of questioning. Of course he would prefer to deal with why Ballard had missed the meeting with Chan and exactly when he planned to seal that deal. Ballard couldn't have planned the ringing of his father's cell phone any better.

"No cell phones at the dinner table." Hudson frowned at his son when the phone rang again.

Daniel had pulled the phone from his hip by then, looking down at it, then frowning up at his father, his gaze softening only when he looked to his mother. "Excuse me. I have to take this call."

When Ballard's father was out of the dining room, Hudson sighed. "That boy still doesn't get it."

"He's had a rough time, Hudson. Daniel's always been one to hold in his true feelings," Leandra said, putting her napkin neatly onto the table.

"That's why his marriage failed," Hudson snapped. "No patience. No commitment to the things that matter most in life."

Ballard had heard all this before, from both his grandfather and his mother. To an extent he agreed: his father was an extremely rigid and most times closed-off man. He loved his business as though he actually expected it to one day love him back. Some might say the same about Ballard, but he didn't agree. He was different because he wasn't foolish enough to make the commitment of marriage or family, knowing that he had the propensity to choose business first. It was one of the smartest and most logical decisions he'd ever made for himself. Obviously, there were some who disagreed.

"I don't want you to make that same mistake, son."

He looked up when he heard his grandfather speaking to him.

"What mistake is that?" he asked when he probably should have simply remained silent.

"Don't make your entire life about this business. There's more out there." Hudson reached his hand across the table, finding his wife's and entwining with it without even looking down. "Find yourself a good wife and build a loving family. That's what all this is about. That's why I worked so hard, so that my family could have something good, something to be proud of. Not so they could use it as an excuse to not live a full life."

"Dad just loves the company, Pops," he replied, always uncomfortable at having to defend his father to his grandfather. "He works so hard because he is proud of what you built."

"He works so hard because he's hiding," Hudson insisted. "Hiding from his failures and defeats. He lost sight of what was important and he's too damned stubborn and proud to admit it."

This time Ballard did remain silent. Debating with Hudson just simply wasn't worth it. The man had his opinion and he would stand by it until the day he died. So Ballard simply picked up his glass and took a slow sip of his wine.

"You're dedicated to the business, as well," Hudson continued.

Ballard nodded. "I am. I think we have a lot of forward movement yet to make. Technology as well as new relationships are going to be a key part to our continued growth in this digital age." Finally, they were on a better subject, a topic Ballard was more comfortable speaking about.

"New relationships," Hudson said with a nod to his wife. "That's just what I'm thinking."

"Don't meddle, Hudson," Leandra warned.

The older man shushed his wife. "Nonsense. It's not meddling where my company is concerned, or my family, for that matter."

Ballard had begun to put his napkin on the table, more than ready to announce his exit, when Hudson's next words stopped him cold.

"The Howertons are from a good, stable stock. Hell, they've got some roots in shipping, which is all right by me," he continued with a light chuckle. "You put some real effort into courting that woman, find yourself some happiness there, maybe even marry her and I'll put you in charge of the company."

Ballard couldn't believe what he'd just heard. "Excuse me?"

Hudson nodded, sitting back in his chair, his ever-rounding belly poking out to signify he'd just had a good, satisfying meal. He'd released his wife's hand to clasp his fingers together over the girth as he looked down the table to Ballard.

"I'm about ready to give up the day-to-day working myself."

"You cut your hours years ago," Ballard added. "I thought you were enjoying your semiretirement."

The older man shrugged. "Might be time to make it a permanent retirement. Leandra and I still have lots we want to do, places I've promised to take her. If I know the company's in good hands, I can do that in peace."

"My dad's doing a great job as CEO." And Ballard had never dreamed of ousting his father from that position. Sure, he figured it would come to him someday, after it had gone through the proper procession—Hudson, Daniel, him—not before.

Hudson didn't agree. "Daniel needs to take a step back, to reevaluate and find himself before he loses everything that's important."

"Pops, that's Dad's battle. We should let him fight it on his own terms," Ballard insisted.

He agreed that his father had grown even more distant since the divorce and, as far as Ballard knew, had not been seriously involved with another woman since then. But just as Ballard felt his personal life was his business, he wanted to offer his father that same respect.

Ballard hadn't expected Hudson to sit forward, slamming his palm on the table so that all the glassware and silverware trembled. "This is my company! I'll run it on my terms!"

"Calm down, Hudson. No need getting your pressure up over things you can't change," Leandra said, going to stand beside her husband with a hand on his shoulder. "Ballard's right—Daniel needs to find his own way."

"Fine. He can do that on his own time," was Hudson's retort. "As for you," he said, pointing at Ballard this time, "I expect better. I want more. Marry that girl and get the corporation you love so much. Can you do that?"

Ballard swallowed, at a loss for words. As good a businessman as he knew he was, Ballard had no idea what type of reply was even called for in a situation like this. He'd just met Janelle Howerton, barely knew her beyond the fact that the kiss they'd shared had haunted him ever since. But that was just physical. There were no feelings involved, no emotional attachments—those weren't his forte. The fact that his grandfather was actually giving him an ultimatum that concerned this woman flabbergasted him.

And then his own cell phone rang, Miles Davis's "Blue in Green" his ringtone. Ballard quickly cleared his throat and reached for his phone. Glancing down at the screen, he saw a number he'd only just programmed in this morning as he'd looked at her website online.

"I have to take this call," he announced to his grandfather's frowning face. "It's Janelle," he added, and watched as that frown quickly receded.

"Well, you'd better answer it, then," Hudson told him, lifting his hand up to meet his wife's on his shoulder.

Ballard stood from the table and headed out of the

dining room to answer the call, wondering what the hell had just happened with his grandparents and, at the same time, what had made the slightly uptight Janelle Howerton decide to call him.

# Chapter 5

Janelle was a Howerton, which meant she was used to certain things—big parties, private schools, lavish houses, the works. Still, when she answered the front door of her family home after the doorbell rang, she was shocked to see the stretch limousine parked in the driveway.

"Janelle Howerton?" the driver, dressed in a black suit, white shirt, gray tie and even a chauffeur's hat, asked.

She had to catch herself as she was still staring at the car, then did an actual double take at the chauffeur.

"Ah, yes. I am. I'll be right with you," she told him as she moved back inside the house to get a jacket and her purse.

It wasn't that she'd never seen or ridden in a limo before. She had, more times than she could remember. This was supposed to be a *simple* dinner date. Unlike her first dinner with Ballard, which she had been adamant was not a date. This made her think back to the last time she'd gone out to dinner with Jack, meeting him at a restaurant and returning to their hotel room alone. That had been the last night she'd seen Jack Trellier, and it hadn't ended well. Besides all that, when she'd called Ballard earlier in the week, she'd suggested dinner over the weekend because she figured it would be easier on both of them since he lived in Boston. His reply had been, "I'll take care of everything and will send you the details in an email on Thursday night."

She'd thought that was a little cryptic. Vicki had said it sounded mysterious and romantic. Sandra had only shrugged and advised her to go with it. That was precisely what Janelle was trying to do as she looked through the tinted windows of the limousine to see that they were slowing down somewhere on a waterfront.

It was a little after eight, so the sky was darkening, lights from nearby buildings casting eerie reflections on the near-black water. When the car stopped completely, Janelle frowned because there was no restaurant in sight. In fact, all the buildings were on the other side of the water.

When the limo door opened, she scooped her jacket and purse from the seat and stepped out into the cool night air. It wasn't officially fall yet, but the evenings had already grown chillier, hence the suit jacket she'd brought to put on over the short-sleeved knee-length royal-blue dress she wore. After closing the door behind her, Janelle noted that the chauffeur, who was überprofessional but just slightly rude because he hadn't said a word other than her name in the past hour they'd been together, had already begun walking ahead of her. She hadn't expected cordial conversation, but she would like some answers.

"I'm supposed to meet Mr. Dubois for dinner. Do you know where he is or why we're here?"

He walked slowly, about two steps ahead of her, his bowed legs reminding Janelle of her father's younger brother who lived in South Carolina. And he did not respond.

She frowned at his back, being careful not to get the heel of her shoe caught in the wood planks of the dock. Had she known she would be walking on a dock, she might have given her wardrobe a little more thought. As it was, she was irritated that she'd taken over an hour to decide what to wear and that now she'd obviously chosen the wrong outfit.

Deep in her own thoughts, Janelle had ceased paying attention to the driver, who wouldn't speak to her anyway. So when he stopped, she wasn't aware, and hence bumped into his back. He didn't move and still did not say a word.

"Excuse me," she muttered, and stepped back.

He turned to the side, then extended an arm, directing her to walk along the plank to his left. The plank that was lined with a black plush material that looked out of place on a shipping dock. She was just about to ask another question when she heard another voice and looked up to see Ballard Dubois standing at the other end of the plank.

"Good evening, Janelle," he said, his voice deep and smooth, reaching the five- to six-foot distance between them to wrap around her as warmly as the jacket in her hand ever could.

A light breeze shifted the edges of his dark suit jacket. His left hand was in his pant pocket and she glimpsed his muscular chest even through the dress shirt and tie. Her mouth watered but she ignored it. "Good evening," she said, taking the steps to close the distance between them.

Once she was near, Ballard reached for her hand and lifted it to his lips for a featherlight kiss. "I am so pleased you could make it tonight."

He smelled like heaven and hell all rolled into one gorgeous package. The scent was intoxicating, strong and powerful, masculine and alluring. In a dream world she could lie against his broad chest inhaling his scent, becoming aroused and enjoying the love-making she was certain he would be skilled at. That would certainly be heaven, which then led to hell, because Janelle had given up on dreams a long time ago. Still, she opened her mouth to speak and had to close it again because the first words to come to her mind were definitely not what she should say to him.

He was holding both her hands by the time Janelle got a grip on her senses and spoke like a woman with a modicum of sense.

"A simple restaurant would have sufficed," she told him. Especially since this second meeting wasn't about anything more than finishing up the political aspect of their relationship. She'd had days to rethink Vicki and Sandra's push that she get to know Ballard better on a personal level. It wasn't a smart move— she knew that.

"Never settle for less," he replied. "Not when you can have the very best."

With those words, Ballard kept one of her hands clasped comfortably in his as he led her onto the deck of his yacht. Looking around, she noted benches with striped cushions, tables with gleaming silver legs and marble tops, a wet bar and a hot tub. In the direction of the stern were more wraparound benches covered in the same striped cushions. That was the direction Ballard walked and she followed.

He led her to the U shape of seats, a small oak table in front of them.

"Have a seat. We'll have a drink while we wait for dinner to be plated," he said.

Everything Ballard said sounded like an instruction, as if he was used to telling people what to do all the time. For a second Janelle thought about being offended. Then she remembered the start of their first dinner together and decided to take his comments and actions a little more lightly this time around. She was certain there were aspects of her demeanor he wasn't thrilled with, as well. And if he knew anything about the real Janelle Howerton, well, they wouldn't be going through this dinner dance at all.

"She's beautiful," she said, taking her seat and putting her things down beside her.

He looked a little surprised, then acknowledged, "Thank you. I've had her for a little more than a year now. I guess you could call her one of my hobbies."

Janelle nodded, trying not to watch the way he confidently moved, picking up the wine bottle, pouring their glasses, handing her one, like a man used to being served but knowing how to serve, as well.

She took a small sip, then said, "My brother, DJ, has similar toys. He's always loved the water, whether swimming or sailing."

"Ah, yes, Darren Howerton Jr., young CEO of Howerton Technologies. He's doing a fantastic job. Your stock is skyrocketing."

He sat on the bench not two feet away from her, his glass in his left hand. His hair was close to his scalp in thick waves, the pecan tone of his skin a perfect accent to the coral-colored tie he wore. His jacket rested excellently over broad shoulders that her fingers itched to touch.

"You've done your research, I see," she added. "Yes, HCT is doing very well."

"But you're not interested in the family company, because you have your own dream. I know Alluring Affairs is doing quite well for itself also. In fact, Harford's still raving about you since his event last week."

"Really?" she asked, almost choking on the sip of wine she'd just taken. "I didn't really do anything for his event except day-of supervision. My friend Rebecca had the entire evening planned right down to the last person of the cleanup crew."

"Well, I'd say you can probably expect more business coming your way. If not from Harford himself, his friends that will surely want to outdo him." Ballard chuckled at that, a warm sound that ended too quickly as another voice interrupted.

"Dinner is served."

Janelle looked to the left, to the man dressed in a tuxedo and tails.

"Shall we?" Ballard asked, standing and extending his hand to her.

Janelle followed him to the lower level, loving the decor of caramel-toned wood on the walls, plush ivory carpet on the floors and warm ivory-and-chocolate furniture throughout.

"Your decorator did a great job," she commented as they walked to the eight-foot dining room table. She was just about to say something else when a familiar scent wafted through the air.

Thank you. I like how it turned out," he was telling her as he pulled out one of the covered chairs for her to sit.

"Is that jasmine?" Janelle asked, unable to shake the instantly relaxing aura the scent elicited for her.

"Yes. The candles."

Ballard nodded toward the two long-stem candles on either side of an overflowing arrangement of pale pink and white orchids.

She looked at him in question and was rewarded by another one of his reach-out-and-grab-you smiles. She sensed he didn't give those often and felt a little privileged at having seen it twice already this evening.

"Your business partners are extremely helpful," he told her. "I simply called your office one day and one of them picked up. The next thing I know, I was inundated with emails detailing what you like and don't like."

"What? Are you serious?" She was going to hurt them, both of them, for meddling and interfering and, she figured finally with a sigh, for being the best friends a woman could ask for.

Ballard chuckled. "Don't be upset with them. I asked for help and they were more than happy to provide it. I got the feeling they wanted you to have a good time tonight."

She knew exactly how good a time they wanted her to have and she still wasn't game, even if the flowers were beautiful, the scented candles that touch of romance she absolutely adored.

"I'm not upset. Still, I'll apologize for them. I haven't dated a lot recently and they just get so carried away."

The man dressed in a tuxedo, whom she might as well go ahead and call the waiter, appeared again, refilling their wineglasses.

"No need for an apology. I'm just glad we're on the same page that tonight is officially a date."

His warm brown eyes pinned her with that statement and Janelle felt like squirming. No, she felt like getting up and going over to his chair to straddle him. She cleared her throat before speaking, using the moment to get her mind right. "I asked you to dinner to talk more about your political involvement and my father's campaign."

The first course was served and Janelle smiled inwardly at the steaming-hot bowl of French-onion soup that was placed before her.

"I'd rather talk about why you haven't dated a lot recently," Ballard countered.

No, she did not want to discuss that and was frankly pissed at herself for mentioning it at all.

"I don't have time," she decided to reply. "You can relate to that, can't you? I mean, you work so much even the tabloids were shocked when you found the time to escort Alaya Bentley to the awards show." Dammit, her mouth was just flapping away tonight with things she did not want to say to this man. To stall it at least for a few moments, she picked up her spoon, dipped it into her soup, then brought it to her mouth.

"Okay," he said, nodding, putting down his spoon, as he'd already taken a taste of his soup. "Since we're obviously both adept at researching, let's just take care of the preliminaries. I dated Alaya for approximately six weeks, which, as I've heard since then, is considered a long-term relationship for me. We are not now, nor were we ever, engaged. I am, as they've printed before, an available bachelor again. Now it's your turn."

To say she was taken aback by his concise statement, which sounded an awful lot like an opening to a board-of-directors meeting, was an understatement.

Still, as much as she wanted to dodge the question once more, she had to admit that she'd opened the door with her comment. She might as well be woman enough to step through it and reply.

"No boyfriend. No recent ex-boyfriend. I've spent the past five years mourning my mother's death, doing whatever I could to help my dad get over the loss and building my business. That's my life and I'm perfectly content with it."

His frown signaled that maybe *he* wasn't. But Janelle didn't care. This was as personal as she wanted things to get between her and Ballard. He was a dangerous man, she'd surmised. From those sexy-as-hell bedroom eyes to the cut of his suit and the scent of his cologne, she wanted him in a physical way that had eluded her for most of her life. Hell, even Jack had called her frigid, no matter how hard she'd tried to please him. Until pleasing him was no longer an option.

She changed the subject and they talked once again about yachts, which eventually circled the conversation back to his shipping business and his plans for the future. And for the next hour Janelle thought, just maybe, she might be safe with Ballard Dubois.

The dinner had been delicious and so filling she thought for sure she'd have to run at least five miles to burn off half the calories she'd consumed. Ballard had made sure every one of her favorite dishes was on full display, even down to dessert—apple cobbler with French vanilla-bean ice cream and a fresh sprig of mint. The chef he'd hired for the evening had done an exceptional job and she'd been more than flattered. So when they moved back up to the top deck and the seats at the bow of the vessel, she was feeling very mellow and admitted to enjoying herself immensely on this first—official—date with him.

Until she heard the music and he asked her to dance.

She knew the voice—Ruben Studdard—and had that very same CD at home and instantly recognized the song. More reasons to remain seated as Ballard stood looking down at her expectantly.

"I know you dance, Janelle. We've done it before."

Janelle remembered. She also remembered being in his arms on another occasion, the night after the costume ball when he'd kissed her senseless and she'd all but floated into her hotel room to have the hottest dreams she'd ever experienced about a man. Yeah, she wasn't really ready for a repeat of that experience.

"I don't think—" she was saying when he took her hand.

He'd hauled her up so fast, her body falling into his so quick, not only could she not finish the sentence, she'd forgotten what the hell she was going to say.

"It's just a dance, Janelle," he told her, his arms going around her waist, holding her close.

At first she planned to resist. Then she figured it was pointless. Not to mention it would make her look childish or needy, neither of which she wanted him to assume. So she flattened her palms against his chest but learned quickly that the feel of strength emanating from him was too much to endure that way. She lifted her arms, wrapping them around his neck instead.

For a few silent seconds they simply swayed to the music, listening to the lyrics of the song—or to the other's rapid heartbeat, she thought with chagrin.

"Did you like our kiss?" he asked out of the blue.

She blinked, then met his gaze, refusing to let him intimidate her on any level. "I've been kissed before," was her candid response to his bold and haughty inquiry.

"Not like that," he replied, leaning in closer. "I've never had a kiss like that."

Janelle opened her mouth to speak but knew the words would never make it out. He was going to kiss her again, she was certain. She felt the urge brewing in the pit of her stomach where it had been all evening as she'd waited for each smile he divulged. She'd wanted to kiss him again. If she were absolutely honest with herself, she'd wanted it about five minutes after the first kiss.

So she took. Hell, she took as much as she possibly could, pulling him closer, opening her mouth wider, sucking his tongue deeper into her mouth. He tasted sweet, like the apples in their dessert. The feel of his hands moving up and down her back set her on fire, reminding her again of that heaven-and-hell comparison she'd made about him the moment she arrived for this date.

The song stopped. Or at least she thought it did, but really she couldn't tell. All she knew was that she was in Ballard's arms and he was kissing her until her nipples hardened, her knees went weak and she could think of nothing else but...more.

## Chapter 6

Ballard wanted Janelle. That was no secret, not to him, anyway. The feel of her soft bottom cupped tightly in his palms was just official verification. A technicality that he didn't need but enjoyed immensely regardless.

When her hands gripped the back of his head and she pushed herself farther into him, he'd had no other choice but to moan in pleasure, taking the kiss deeper, needing more, faster. Acting purely on instinct and desire, he took a step forward, his hands going down her thighs, lifting her. He tore his lips from hers only long enough to lay her on the cushioned bench and climb on top of her. Then his mouth was on her again, kissing the line of her jaw, trailing a path down her neck. She'd spread her legs and he reached for one thigh and hiked it up to his waist, thrusting his arousal against the warmth of her juncture.

He'd never made love to a woman on his yacht. Never hired a chef to cook all the things a woman favored. Never cared enough to go to the trouble of flowers, candles, music. Yet this time, this first official date, he had. The question of why was echoing in his mind, had been all day long, but he'd pushed it away.

A week ago he'd never met Janelle Howerton, and while sex had always been a favored pastime of his, he'd never imagined or experienced wanting of this magnitude.

On the flip side of this thirst for sexual pleasure— a thirst that threatened to cause him grave physical pain—there was the ultimatum. His grandfather had candidly said if he married Janelle Howerton— a woman he'd just met—he would be named CEO of the company he'd wanted to run all his life.

As a rule, Ballard didn't like threats or ultimatums or anyone who believed they could intimidate him into doing their bidding. He was his own man; he walked his own path, did his own thing. He did not, as much as the prize meant to him, take orders from someone else—even his grandfather, whom he loved and respected a great deal.

Beneath him Janelle arched her back, her breasts pressing firmly into his chest. His kisses went lower, dipping beneath the collar of her dress to the swell of said breasts. He licked the smooth skin there, loved the softness, the sweet enticing aroma of her perfume.

He whispered her name. She sighed, "Yes." And for the first time since he was thirteen years old, Ballard thought he might actually find his release in his pants.

He paused then, closing his eyes, then reopening them. Pulling back slightly, he looked down at Janelle, at her kiss-swollen lips, passion-filled eyes and ruffled dress. And he cursed.

In the next seconds, he was moving until he was sitting at least three feet away from her on the bench, staring forward to the water as he heard her moving beside him. She was adjusting her clothes, sitting upright, trying to control her breathing, trying to figure out what the hell they'd been doing. The latter he'd been working on himself, cursing the fact that he'd actually been on his way to freeing his erection and sinking into her waiting heat.

"I apologize," he said softly. "That was out of line."

She cleared her throat, finally going still on the bench. He thought about looking at her, making eye contact so that she knew he was sincere about his apology, but he couldn't. Desire still tore through him like a mighty wind. His fingers still itched to touch her, his tongue to taste her. He closed his eyes, attempting to clear that fog from his mind once more. This hesitation, these recriminations were not his normal routine with females.

"We're consenting adults, Ballard. There's no need to apologize for something we both wanted," she told him.

He did look to her then, surprised at her words since she'd been the one drawing a clear line between their attraction and a platonic acquaintance. Maybe he wasn't the only one grappling with personal contradictions tonight.

"I'm not usually like this with women," he admitted.

Ballard wasn't sure why the urge to be brutally honest with her was so strong. Sure, he prided himself on setting the parameters early for his relationships, but this, what he was saying to her, was different. It was as if he needed to remind himself of how far he should and should not go.

"I set the tone. I lay out the rules. She either accepts or she doesn't." He shrugged. "Either way, I walk away completely intact."

"And that works for you?" she asked, her tone incredulous. "The strict rules and limitations are always agreeable?"

Leaning forward, he rested his elbows on his knees, still unable to look at her.

"It's what I do," he replied simply.

"Like your job? Your contribution to society? Your privilege?"

She was angry—he could tell by the rise in her voice. He didn't want her to be, but he didn't want her to feel misled either. He stood then, slipping his hands into his pockets and looking down at her. "I believe in being up-front, letting people know where they stand. Is that a crime? Or would you rather I lie to you, lead you on and then break your heart?"

That was when she stood, taking the extra steps to face him directly. She was a tall woman, with terrific legs and shoulders that squared when she was angry, eyes that flared when she was about to lay down the law.

"The only way you could break my heart, Ballard Dubois, is if I let you, which, for the record, I have no intention of doing," she stated coolly. "Is that up-front enough for you?"

Ballard smiled. He couldn't help it. She was so damned sexy, so alluring. Her voice, the movement of her lips, the tilt of her head… He desired her like he'd never wanted another female in his life before.

"I believe that's a fair statement," he replied.

She nodded. "Good. I'm ready to leave now."

He nodded in agreement, not really ready for her to leave but knowing it was best, tonight, for both of them.

That night Janelle dreamed of his hands on her breasts, cupping them, squeezing them. His lips on her nipples, suckling, then clasping them lightly with his teeth. She sucked in a breath, arched her back and pressed her palms against the back of his head, edging him forward, loving the sensations rippling through her body as he did.

When one of his hands left her aching breasts to slide down the torso, over her belly and farther still to her smoothly shaved juncture, she sighed. Her legs parted willingly, impatiently. His fingers explored her folds, peeling them back like petals to a flower, finding her swollen bud inside. Her body trembled, her teeth sinking into her bottom lip. He pressed two fingers there, rotating them in a circular fashion until her breathing hitched and a gasp escaped. When her thighs shook uncontrollably at his ministrations, she whispered his name.

"Ballard."

His reply was instant, an urgent murmur. "Yes, Janelle, yes."

The words instantly went into replay, convincing her that yes was the answer, that giving her all to this man was the key, that surrender would not be the end but the beginning.

Then the tenderness shifted. The room that had been warm with a slight breeze coming off the bay, the scent of salt water tickling her nostrils, was now cold, foreboding. The voice that spoke to her this time was neither smooth nor deep. It was frightening.

"Open your eyes," he ordered. "Watch while I teach you what pleasure is."

Her eyes shot open, even though she knew it was a mistake.

The man looming above her wasn't six-plus feet tall with a darker skin tone and dreamy brown eyes. He wasn't wearing an expertly tailored suit or that enticing cologne. He didn't look at her with clear confidence and the sense that she was the only woman in the world.

No, this was not Ballard.

It was Jack and he was hurting her, again.

"No!" she screamed, instantly bucking up her knees to kick him away.

He slapped her then, so hard the tingling traveled

from her cheek to her eye sockets, down to the roots of her teeth, the tips of her toes. Before she could rebound, his hand was between her legs, pushing, breaching, forcing.

Janelle screamed. She swung her arms, landing slaps against the side of his head, his back, his arms. She fought him every step of the way. Yelling for him to stop, to get away from her, until finally he pulled away.

"You're a stuck-up bitch! Always have been, walking around campus teasing every guy that was foolish enough to look your way. But when it really comes down to it, you're just a silly little girl, Janelle Howerton," he spat. "A silly, naive girl that's too frigid and uptight to know how to please a man. And I'm tired of trying to teach you, trying to wait for you to grow up and get with the program. There are too many other females out there just waiting to give me whatever I want, whenever I want it."

His words had been harsh, like tiny blades pricking at her skin. She'd huddled on the bed, curling into a fetal position for the first half of his little speech. Then when he'd called her silly and naive, she'd leaped off the bed, reaching for the lamp on the nightstand. She yanked the cord from the wall, holding it comfortably in her palm, ready to swing again if his little tirade was going to shift to the physical again. Her other hand fisted at her side, she was so angry, so betrayed, so hurt.

She didn't speak, hadn't said a word, simply stared

him down, letting him know that she was ready, waiting for him to make another move.

He didn't.

Jack Trellier and his 3.8 grade point average, his bright and shining future as the new head of Trell Cosmetics, his butter complexion and light green eyes, walked out of her bedroom and out of her life.

Jerking up in the bed, Janelle pulled her sheets to her neck, her breathing erratic, eyes searching the bedroom she'd used on the Howerton estate since she'd been born. She blinked and blinked again, breathed until she was calm, until the demons that liked to invade her sleep periodically were gone. Then she lay back and cried, tears warm and steady streaming down her face, falling to her pillow.

## *Chapter* 7

Janelle stopped walking. She took a step back and glanced at the newsstand once more. Her heart had begun a stilted rhythm in her chest and her eyes blinked repeatedly, most likely in the hopes of convincing her that what she thought she saw wasn't possible. Luckily, she wore dark shades, so the other customers in the convenience store where she'd stopped to pick up a pack of gum and an iced tea in lieu of lunch wouldn't notice her staring or her disbelief.

Finally, she picked up the magazine, gasping, as close up, the picture looked even more intimate than she'd known it to be—if that were even possible. The caption beneath the picture stated "See more inside," so she flipped through the glossy pages, her stomach twisting the moment she looked down to her own smiling face. She closed her eyes then, whispering every prayer she could think of before reopening them.

It was no use. She was still in the picture, her arms wrapped around Ballard's neck as she stared up at him wantonly. Yes, wantonly, dammit! Her hands shook as she continued to hold the magazine, stuck standing absolutely still in that spot. Until someone bumped her from behind.

"Oh, I read that entire article. They make a lovely couple, don't you think?" the older lady wearing a large-brimmed black hat with a bright red cardinal on the right side said to her with a smile.

Janelle had to force her own smile in return. Hell, she had to prompt herself to speak in return.

"I don't really know. Does the article say they're a couple?" she asked, ever thankful for the Ray-Ban Jackie O sunglasses that were a birthday gift from Sandra.

The woman waved a jewel-clad hand, her purse slipping back on her arm as she moved. "Well, you know, it says 'unofficial' but just look at them, all tangled up together. I always feel like it's watching our own version of royalty when Bostonians fall in love. Just think, the Howertons are about to be political superstars and the Dubois are shipping monarchs. You know, I went to school with Leandra Dubois. She's a dear."

The woman said more, something about a lavish Boston wedding with politicians and movie stars and babies, and Janelle wanted to scream, or faint, whichever was more inconspicuous. Knowing neither was realistic, she gingerly placed the magazine back on the stand and wished the older lady a nice day. Then she got the hell out of that store, reaching into her purse to find her cell phone so she could call Sandra or Vicki or both of them and ask if anyone in Wintersage had seen that magazine. Both of them were out of the office and not answering their cells and she was now going to be late if she didn't hustle to meet Everley Madison.

Everley was an anxious bride-to-be who had requested an over-the-top glitz-and-glam wedding to take place on New Year's Eve. She was a new client who had attended the Harford charity event and had traced Janelle through calls to Rebecca's office. Since Rebecca was still out of town, Everley had insisted Janelle handle her wedding. Never one to turn down new business, no matter how busy she already was, Janelle had scheduled the Friday meeting and made her way up to Boston.

Now the heels of her black suede booties clicked along the brick sidewalks of Boston's historic Beacon Hill. She was meeting Everley at one of the antiques shops on Charles Street because there was a chandelier that she wanted to use for the reception. Janelle tried to clear her mind of the magazine and the suggestion that she and Ballard were "Boston's new sweethearts," as the headline had touted. She focused instead on business, on sharing the ideas and thoughts she'd been able to come up with for Everley's big day. The thrill of a new event rippled through her as she crossed the street, a small smile playing on her lips. She saw the limousine parked in front of the shop where she was meeting Everley but didn't pay it much attention. Actually, she figured it was Everley's since the twenty-three-year-old pop singer had just released her second platinum CD.

"Yaay!" Everley squealed the moment Janelle walked into the quaint little shop.

She ran to Janelle, all ninety-five pounds of female with golden-blond hair hanging in deep waves to her butt, piercings in her nose, her bottom and top lips, and her eyebrow, and the really-small-but-still-there chipped diamond that twinkled from the corner of her mouth.

"Hello," Janelle said, going into the embrace but not really steadying herself for Everley's body slamming into hers. She stumbled back just a step, then centered herself with a chuckle. "It's good to see you again."

Janelle hadn't really talked to Everley at the Harford party—more like she'd been introduced and Everley's attention had stayed fixated on the drink in her hand and the gorgeous guy on her arm. Still, the moment she received the call about this lavish and highly publicized wedding, Janelle had immediately thanked Rebecca and begun working. She'd been doing double time at Alluring Affairs with the homecoming dance just around the corner and Everley's requests clogging her inbox and her cell phone. This meeting was to get some things set in concrete so they could move forward with the fast-approaching event that was sure to be touted as one of the most talked-about of the upcoming year.

"It's right over here and it's gorgeous!" Everley continued, excitement edging her voice as she moved back the few feet until she was once again standing right next to the chandelier.

Janelle had to admit, of all the things she'd expected from today's visit, this wasn't it. Between Everley's party-girl persona, her sexually explicit music and her future husband, an NBA player who was fire on the court and a ticking time bomb on the streets, she thought she might have a very stressful job on her hands. But as she moved closer, reaching out to touch the bronze-colored crystals that made up this most unique piece, she could do nothing but smile.

"It's gorgeous," she told Everley.

"It's something called Golden Teak Strass crystal. That's what he said," Everley commented with a wave of her hand toward someone who Janelle suspected was the owner of the shop.

He was a tall, thin man, his face weathered and patient as he stood to the side, Everley's bodyguards standing near the front door and a staff-only door to the back of the shop.

"It costs 7,000," the man added in a surprisingly strong voice.

"I already told you price doesn't matter. I've got this," Everley said with a roll of her eyes. She hadn't even turned back to look at the owner as she'd replied.

Janelle glanced at the older man and offered a conciliatory smile.

"So this is the design idea you want to follow?" she asked Everley. "It's elegant and this color is very unique."

"Right! That's what I want—elegant and unique. I want every guest to remember this wedding for the rest of their lives," she continued. "I want my gown to be this color, too, and everyone else will wear ecru. It'll be gorgeous."

She was right about that, Janelle thought with even more surprise. At the office she'd come up with some preliminary ideas based on Everley's and her fiancé's personalities. Standing here, she realized her thoughts had been totally off.

Janelle was nodding while Everley continued to look at the chandelier. "I have the perfect venue in mind. You said you liked flowers. I think you should have them everywhere. And I know the perfect designer for your dress. She's up-and-coming, drew up quite a buzz last spring at New York's Fashion Week. You'll be the first in Hollywood to wear one of her uniquely designed couture gowns."

Everley was practically glowing for the rest of their forty-minute conversation, which took place while the store owner wrapped the chandelier in plastic and carefully boxed it for shipment. By the time the bodyguards came to Everley, reminding her of another engagement, Janelle was flushed with excitement. The adrenaline rush of a new event, of the new possibilities, of a large glamorous wedding, always did this to her. It gave her a sense of purpose and a surge of energy that she didn't experience in any other aspect of her life. Her father could have politics. Her brother could have the family business with his suits and ties and stuffy business meetings. As for her, she loved her job!

That said, she was generally used to things not quite going according to plan. She prided herself on remaining calm and dealing professionally with whatever was thrown her way during an event. But then, *this* surprise, the one she was faced with as she walked out of the shop and saw the passenger door of the limo, the one parked there when she came in, open.

The distance between the entrance of the shop and the curb was less than ten feet, and coming out of the limo door, shoes were visible first, black tie-ups. As both feet hit the redbrick sidewalk, her gaze continued upward to cuffed black dress pants, pleated, and a black suit jacket with the faintest gray stripe. A crisp stone-gray dress shirt with a black-and-gray paisley-print tie. The suit jacket rested on his shoulders, strong broad shoulders, and her pulse skipped a beat. Ballard's shape-up and goatee were precisely cut, as if he'd just walked away from the barber's chair. His strong hands moved softly down the lapels of his jacket as he stepped away from the door, looking at her with the barest hint of a smile.

Janelle couldn't move. She didn't know what to say. It had been days since she'd heard from him, and actually, she hadn't thought she would again. After their dinner on his yacht and the uncomfortable way in which it ended, she'd figured whatever physical thing had been between them had fizzled. Yesterday morning she'd sent him an email outlining her father's campaign and requesting his support. Her father had asked her to do something for him and she wasn't about to let a little lapse in judgment stop her from at least trying to see the job through. Ballard hadn't responded and she'd figured that was it.

Now, as her breasts felt full with desire, telltale throbbing starting between her legs, she knew she'd been wrong. The physical tug, the desire, the need, was still there. With a damned vengeance.

"It's nice to see you again, Janelle," he said after he'd closed the distance between them and now stood directly in front of her.

"What are you doing here?" was Janelle's instant question. "Are you following me?"

It seemed like a crazy question to ask but Ballard Dubois was a busy man. She doubted very seriously that he'd wanted to buy an antique today of all days, or that he'd sit in this car for almost an hour waiting to do so.

His lips spread into that grin that was like a stroke of heat licking along her body.

"Not following you, but definitely tracking you down so I could see you."

"That's the same thing."

He shook his head. "Maybe. Maybe not."

"I'm working, Ballard," she said, attempting to move around him.

"You're finished with your meeting for the day. You only came to Boston to meet with this client and then you're slated to head right back home. I called your office," he added when she opened her mouth to ask how he knew her schedule.

"Your partners told me where you would be after I indicated how desperately I needed to see you."

"Desperately?" She chuckled. "Ballard, we had a date, we made out a little and we let it go. It was out of the ordinary for both of us, remember?"

He lifted a hand then, cupping her face right there in the middle of the sidewalk. Janelle immediately remembered the pictures she'd seen in the magazine, the allegations that she and Ballard were a couple, and she stepped back.

"Don't," she whispered, turning her head away from his.

He paused, then cleared his throat. "I wanted to see you. I've wanted to see you for the past few days. I couldn't wait any longer."

"You didn't call," she told him without looking at him. "You didn't respond to my email."

"We don't always make the right decisions at the right time," he continued. "I'm here now, exactly where I want to be. Join me for dinner."

Janelle was already shaking her head. "I don't want to be in the tabloids. I don't want people taking pictures of me and making assumptions about my life. I don't want any of this," she said in one breath, and felt as if she'd purged herself.

She looked at him then, squaring her shoulders

and taking a deep breath. "Whatever you can do for my father's campaign would be greatly appreciated."

Janelle's next words were cut off as Ballard came closer, this time cupping her face in both hands and pulling her to him so that their bodies were touching. When his lips crashed down over hers, she lost all sense of time and place and thought and…everything but him. His scent, his touch, his taste.

She was simply…lost.

Dinner wasn't what Janelle had anticipated. Not only had it not been in her original plan for the evening, but she'd never expected Ballard to show up or to take her to this place, of all the restaurants in Boston.

The limousine pulled up in front of Area Four, a restaurant in the Kendall Square area of Cambridge. Ballard ushered her into the casual dining venue, where they ordered the best Hawaiian pizza Janelle had ever tasted. Their dinner was made complete with the orange-chocolate s'more with chocolate ice-cream sundae they shared like two high school students sitting in a '50s malt shop.

After dinner Ballard directed the limo to drive her home to Wintersage. When she protested, stating that she'd parked her car just a few blocks from the antiques shop, he insisted on having her car brought to her in the morning. As night had fallen and the past few hours had been some of the best times she'd ever had, Janelle wasn't in the mood to argue.

Ballard's hand clasped hers, his fingers entwining

with her own as they sat in the backseat of the limo. She accepted the warmth of his grasp, hadn't even argued about how close he'd sat to her on the quiet ride back. She was tired, had been experiencing one nightmare after another each time she closed her eyes at night, so sleep hadn't come easily in the past few days. Her head lolled back on the seat and she looked out the window.

"I don't know where this is going," he said. "That's difficult for me to say considering I like having all the facts, knowing the complete lay of the land before I explore."

That sounded like him. Always in control, always doing the right thing. Ballard wouldn't have lied to his family and friends, as she had.

"What I know for sure right at this moment is that I want to keep seeing you. I want us to continue getting to know each other."

"Is that the prelude into the next stage of dating? Does that mean we can have sex now?" The words were out before Janelle could think them through, the tinge of anger that had lingered every morning after she'd climbed from her bed lacing every syllable.

For his part, Ballard didn't flinch at the coolness of her questions. He didn't release her hand, nor did he budge.

"It's a statement of fact. An undeniable one. I want to continue seeing you, Janelle. It's as simple as that."

Nothing in life was simple. Nothing where a man and a woman were concerned was cut-and-dried. She'd learned that long ago, when she'd given her heart, her trust, her everything and had gotten slapped down and kicked to the side in return. Instinct once again told Janelle to bolt, to run for her life, for her sanity, for her protection. But instinct was stalled as Ballard's thumb moved slowly over the back of her hand.

"You're a strong woman, Janelle. You're a decisive businesswoman and a good daughter. Fear is not in your makeup. It's not who or what you are."

She was shaking her head as he spoke. "You don't know me. Don't sit there and talk to me like you know me."

"I know that you're as interested in getting to know me as I am you. I know that whatever is growing between us is not casual and it's not dwindling."

"You know everything, don't you, Ballard?"

He pulled her closer to him then, touching a finger to her chin and turning her to face him. "I know that I want you. Can you honestly deny the same?"

She couldn't. Janelle knew the moment she'd climbed into his limo this afternoon that she couldn't deny what was brewing between them. The magazine, the memories, the election—none of that changed what was. Ballard was right: she prided herself on being intelligent and strong and courageous—she'd had to be. Could she really deny him? Could she now deny what was so obviously there?

"What we want is not always what we need," was her response.

"Then let me give you what you need, Janelle. Let me give you what you deserve."

It was an honest plea, she thought. A very sincere admission and request and her heart beat so fast she thought it might beat right out of her chest. Her breath caught as she opened her mouth to speak, the words falling away like ashes in the wind.

"Kiss me," she whispered. "Kiss me, Ballard."

And he did. He kissed her until the memories just about faded, the worries and concerns for her emotional safety drifting into the backdrop. She kissed him back with all the abandon, all the time she'd felt had been wasted, loving the feel of his strength beneath her hands, his lips on hers.

When finally the limousine pulled up in front of the house she'd grown up in and still shared with her father, Janelle decided to take a chance, to make a move and pray for the best.

"I've been planning the Wintersage homecoming dance for the past few weeks," she began.

Ballard held her hand as he walked her to the front door. She'd given him her house key before getting out of the car, so he was now poised to unlock the door for her and to escort her inside.

She stopped just inside the dark foyer, turning to look at him. He stood in the doorway, the glow from the moonlight casting a romantic outline around him.

"I'm sure it'll be a wonderful event. You're a very talented event planner. I could tell by how happy that singer looked earlier today after your meeting."

She smiled. "Thank you. But I wasn't fishing for compliments. I was actually going to ask you to be my date to the homecoming dance."

Ballard didn't instantly respond. Instead he stared at her, almost incredulously. That made her nervous and thoughts of making a mistake or moving too fast threatened to absorb her.

Then Ballard's lips lifted into a grin, his straight white teeth bright in the darkness. "I don't think I've ever been asked to a homecoming dance," he told her, and then stepped closer, lacing his arms around her waist.

She was becoming quite comfortable in this position, wrapped in Ballard's arms. "Well, maybe you should provide an answer," she replied, snuggling up to him because the action was so irresistible.

"Yes," he whispered, lowering his forehead to hers. "Yes, Janelle Howerton, I would love to take you to the homecoming dance."

## Chapter 8

Janelle felt like Cinderella going to the ball, only in her fairy tale her Prince Charming had come to the house to pick her up. He was early, as she'd requested since she was both working and attending tonight's dance. The traditional limo had been swapped with an Escalade SUV limo, white, the perfect contrast to Ballard, who was dressed in black slacks, a black collarless shirt and a black dinner jacket.

As for her, there was no long billowy white dress and crystal slippers. Instead Janelle also wore all black, as she tended to do when she worked an event. Her staff, the event assistants she kept on payroll to help with day-of preparations, would also be wearing black. She'd mentioned this to Ballard yesterday when they'd had lunch because, for whatever reason, he'd been in Wintersage unannounced.

"Dressing like the staff, Mr. Dubois," she said once they were on their way to the school. "Be careful— the press might get wind of this and think you're stepping down from Dubois Maritime."

She joked about the press, about the stories that had been hitting the tabloids and local papers on an almost-daily basis now. Janelle never saw a photographer or reporter, but everywhere she and Ballard went, even when they'd sat quietly on the back veranda of her family home, looking out at the sunset on the bay, someone had been there, watching, snapping pictures. Vicki and Sandra thought it was good for business. Her father was ecstatic with the implications of the two families joining, his mind focused solely on the election and the seeming inevitability that he would get the backing of Dubois Maritime.

As for Janelle, she was just coping. She'd decided not to let it dictate her actions, to not give in to the pressure to please the world that in the end didn't give a damn about her on a personal level. She'd decided to simply enjoy how things were progressing with Ballard. The comfortable smile he gave her in return and his next comment confirmed Ballard was on board with that decision.

"I don't care what they print. The truth rarely sells."

She agreed and when they arrived at the Wintersage Academy, they headed inside to the gymnasium where she'd spent so many of her teenage days.

Wintersage Academy was made up of three main buildings and two dormitories—one for boys and the other for girls. The largest and by far the stateliest structure on the campus was the Great Hall, where all the administrative offices and the main function hall were housed. The building was surrounded by lush green grass and tall trees, while lively lavender hydrangea bushes skirted around the perimeter. The hydrangea were bright and cheerful in early spring, gracing the building with their beauty well into the summer. But as fall began its descent on Wintersage, the hydrangea would die off until the next year and all the leaves on all the trees would turn into the glorious golds and reds of the season—which, by the way, was Janelle's absolute favorite time of year.

They walked along the brick path until arriving at the steps topped by eight bright white pillars that Janelle used to think of as bars keeping them inside the school and away from the world. The white double doors were already open, leading the way into the foyer, already awash with the orange and white twinkle lights her staff had hung earlier today. The colors shimmered against the stark white walls marked with evenly distributed pictures of Wintersage dignitaries and glistened over the highly polished honey-colored hardwood floors. Her heels clicked against those floors as they stepped inside and Janelle paused.

"You okay?" Ballard asked, touching a hand to her elbow.

"Fine," she replied, her voice small, unsure. She was fine. This was silly. And by *this,* she meant the icy tendril slipping ever so slowly down her spine and the heated sense of dread that circled her stomach. What was this about?

She cleared her throat, then took a breath and began walking again. "The entrance to the hall is just down here and around the corner. I should go into the back area to check on the caterers. Guests should begin arriving in the next forty-five minutes. The Parents' Association will be here in about fifteen."

When she looked over at Ballard, he was nodding while she talked.

"Am I babbling?"

"Not at all. I believe you're working," he offered with a smile.

She groaned. "Is that bad since I asked you to be my date?"

Ballard chuckled, wrapping his arm around her shoulders and pulling her close. "Remember who you're talking to here. If my cell rings right now with news about the Chan deal, I'll be heading back outside to take it. So, no, it's not bad that you're working. In fact, what can I do to help?"

"What?" she asked.

Before he could answer, a woman's voice interjected. "Oh, there you are. We've been wondering when you would get here. There's a problem with the caterer and the approved menu," Brenda, mother of two, wife to the chief of police, said as she rounded the corner and came face-to-face with Janelle and Ballard.

"Ah, okay, thanks, Brenda," Janelle said as Brenda's gaze shifted.

The fifty-something-year-old woman who swore the part-time work Janelle had offered her was the current joy of her life lit up like a Christmas tree as her gaze settled on Ballard. "Well, well, well. We wondered when we'd get to see you for ourselves. All the pictures in the papers don't do you justice. Great catch!" she said, finally turning back to Janelle with a wink of her eye.

Janelle bit back a moan.

"You go with me to check on the caterer, Brenda," Janelle said in her employer voice. "Ballard, if your offer still stands, could you go inside and check to make sure the entertainment is ready to go and there are no fires in that room that I need to put out at the moment."

She'd already begun digging down into the top of her blouse, searching for the earpiece she'd dropped there before leaving the house. As she pulled it free and tucked it into her ear, she looked to Ballard, who seemed to have been frozen in his spot, his gaze on her breasts.

"It's easier if we can all communicate with each other," she said tapping her ear, then pointing at the identical mechanism in Brenda's ear. "I'll be in the back. Call me on my cell if something's wrong."

He didn't speak, only nodded.

Brenda chuckled all the way to the back where the caterers were getting set up, mumbling about sexy, virile young men and what she used to be able to do with them.

Janelle tried to focus on the event and not on Brenda's inappropriate remarks.

She did not give the reservations or the leeriness she'd felt upon entering the Great Hall another thought. Maybe she should have.

Janelle looked fantastic.

Ballard had spent most of the night watching her move throughout the large room with confidence and efficiency. He was beyond impressed with how calm she seemed as she balanced minor issues and worked through the big ones of the caterer bringing some of the wrong food and the building not providing enough electricity for Candice Glover's band to plug in all their equipment.

She talked with clever enthusiasm, accepted compliments, gave out a few of her own and found moments to stand in the corner and laugh with her girlfriends, the way Ballard suspected she had when they were younger. He'd finally had the opportunity to meet Sandra Woolcott and Vicki Ahlfors and watched the love and loyalty between the three of them with envy. He'd never forged any close friendships while growing up, never thought there was a need. He'd known where he was going in life, known what his job would be and how he would be successful at it. There hadn't seemed to be a need for friends or emotional entanglements of any kind.

Until now.

All night he'd been able to find her wherever she was throughout the room, refused to let her out of sight. Even when the clever and interminably curious women of Wintersage came to pump him for information about his relationship with Janelle, he'd still tracked her, his body adding an unfamiliar emotional response to the physical he'd grown accustomed to.

The room was still surprisingly full for the past half hour of the event. In the middle of the dance floor, members he now knew were from the infamous Parents' Association, the same people who had given Janelle a hard time since she began planning this event, danced and laughed. Ballard smiled smugly as if he'd had something to do with the fact that they were so obviously enjoying the evening. Later he planned to report to Janelle how great a job she'd done and how he'd seen with his own eyes the shock and pleasure of the citizens of this quaint little town at her accomplishment.

There were some other things he hoped to share with her tonight that didn't include anything about this event or the phenomenal entertainment or the food or... Ballard paused. His gaze focused across the room to where Janelle had just walked down the winding staircase that led to the balcony section of the hall. The sound technicians were up there and she periodically went up to make sure everything was working well since they'd had to compromise on the electrical hookups.

Janelle stopped at the last step, her hand gripping the railing. She stared straight ahead toward the door, her entire body going tense. Ballard followed her gaze and felt a wave of jealousy so high and mighty he might have gasped if he weren't in a room full of people.

She was staring at a man. A tall and debonair-looking man who was gaining other stares and whispers as he moved through the crowd. In fact, as this stranger walked across the floor, the dancing ceased, women and men moving to the side to let him through. Overly dramatic and slightly pathetic, Ballard thought, his feet were already carrying him in Janelle's direction.

Ballard stopped right beside her just as the newcomer stepped in front of her.

"Janelle," the man said in a low, almost-intimate voice.

"Jack," she replied, her voice a little shaky to Ballard's ears. "What the hell are you doing here?"

"It's homecoming, remember? You said you always wanted me to take you to a homecoming dance." With those words, Jack reached for Janelle's free hand, bringing it up to his mouth in preparation for a kiss. She yanked it away and brought it back quickly to land with a loud slap against Jack's cheek.

The room went totally silent. Jack frowned. Vicki and Sandra suddenly appeared at Janelle's other side. And Ballard stood wondering what the hell was going on.

Janelle moved as fast as she could out of the hall, away from the staring and the whispering. Her heart thumped wildly in her chest, her eyes stinging as she blinked repeatedly.

"Just chill. He's here—so what?" Sandra was saying as they made their way out into the hallway with her.

"So what?" Vicki chimed in. "Did you see how he walked right up to her and tried to touch her? He's got a lot of nerve."

"Assholes normally do," Sandra added. "But she fixed him good with that slap."

All the while Janelle paced a little path back and forth. She used a hand to fan her instantly flushed face. Why was he here? She'd asked him that and he'd replied. A true but totally inappropriate answer that she'd wanted to stuff right back down his smug-looking mouth. She hated him! No. She hated what he'd done to her. And lately, she'd hated how long she'd allowed his actions to rule what she had become.

"Janelle?"

At the sound of his voice, she stopped pacing.

"We need to talk," Jack told her.

"The hell you do," Sandra insisted, stepping in front of Janelle. "The time for talking has long since passed. You knew when you boarded that plane and left her two weeks before your wedding. That's when you should have been man enough to talk. Now you need to be smart enough to leave."

Vicki stood right beside Sandra, creating a barrier in front of Janelle. Protecting her as they'd done since the breakup. Unfortunately, they had no idea what they were really protecting her from. And Janelle didn't want the protection anyway. She wasn't going to hide from Jack and she wasn't going to avoid him. Way too much of her life had been given to this man involuntarily and it was time for that to end.

She stepped around her friends, looking at both of them. "Give us a minute, please?" she requested, and when they stared back questioningly, she nodded her consent.

"We'll get Ballard," Vicki announced as they moved away slowly.

Janelle didn't reply, had barely heard Ballard's name as she looked at Jack, the man she'd been madly in love with and wanted to marry and have babies with just five years ago.

He looked exactly the same. No, he looked better. His butter-toned complexion highlighted by unique green-hazel eyes. His strong jaw decorated with a thin-cut beard to match the close cut of his sandy-brown-colored hair. He was six feet three inches tall, had played basketball in high school and college and spoke three foreign languages as fluently as if he hadn't been born in Naples, Florida.

There was a certain quality that Jack Trellier possessed, an aura that followed him around like a shadow. At first glance he was the successful athlete, the ladies' magnet and possible catch of the century, heir to the Trell Cosmetics fortune, the gorgeous face of a multibillion-dollar corporation. Then there was the truth, the man beneath the glamour, the person Janelle knew all too well.

"I asked why you are here. I'll give you sixty seconds to respond," she said without flinching.

Her entire body was shaking, whether with anger or a touch of fear, Janelle didn't know and wasn't in the mood to analyze. Tonight had been going so well. The party that had paid her a good fee but had been somewhat of a thorn in her side for the past five weeks had come to a successful culmination, the mayor and the president of the Parents' Association giving her their gratitude and already making hints about next year.

To top that off, her date had been the gorgeous Ballard Dubois. He'd been attentive to her every need, checking on whatever she asked him to do, standing quietly beside her as she talked with the mayor, the chief of police, a reporter from the *Wintersage Journal*. While they hadn't had time to dance, or to eat, for that matter, she'd known he was there and had appreciated every second of his support.

"You've made quite a name for yourself," was Jack's deliberately slow response. "I remember a time when you hated publicity, hated how your name was always linked to your father's, to the company. You wanted a more normal existence, a quieter life filled with success and money and those girlfriends that stuck to you like glue." He chuckled then, letting his head fall back as if he'd recited the funniest joke of the century.

"Is that your answer to my question?" She had no patience where Jack was concerned. At one point, that had been no resistance, no backbone, no self-respect. Now things had drastically changed.

His laughter stopped, the gleam in his eyes still there. He lifted a long arm out, his fingers touching her, tweaking her nose the way he'd always done. She slapped his hand away.

"You've grown a little more violent over the years," he quipped.

"Maybe if I'd been more violent five years ago, you wouldn't be standing here right now," she spat, then sighed. This wasn't her, trembling with rage, shaking with the urge to do more than slap this person who stood before her.

"Still clinging to the past, I see." Jack sighed. "Look, I just came for a visit. I've been reading a lot about you in the papers lately and felt the urge to see you face-to-face."

He looked her up and down then, his sickeningly hot gaze raking over her body as if he knew precisely what was beneath the black slacks and sheer-sleeved black blouse she wore. Her ankles shook slightly in the four-inch-heeled pumps she wore.

"You're wasting my time," she told him. "This visit is over."

Janelle moved around him and he surprisingly stepped to the side to let her past. Then his voice stopped her.

"Does he know how afraid of sex you are? Does he have any idea how unsatisfied you'll leave him night after night? Maybe I should tell him."

Janelle moved ever so slowly, turning around until

she could look into his conniving, lying, despicable face once more.

"You are a vile son of a bitch and if you ever come near me again, I'll make you pay for five years ago and every day you've been blessed to breathe since then. Do I make myself clear, Jack?"

He folded one arm over his chest, lifting the other to rub a finger along his bearded chin. "That sounds like a threat, Janelle. I wonder if I should be afraid. But what are you going to do, run and tell your father some overly dramatic story of our breakup five years ago? Are you going to tell him and your precious friends how you lied to them? Are you going to risk your precious reputation with a story no one is ever going to believe?"

"No," came another male voice from behind Janelle. "Right now she's going to return to this party and dance with her date. Do you have a problem with that, Mr. Trellier?"

Janelle didn't turn around. She couldn't. Ballard's voice sounded so commanding, so authoritative as he came to stand beside her. His arm slipped around her waist so seamlessly, as if there were no other place it could possibly reside. The sigh she released and the instinctive lean into him her body did of its own accord seemed natural, welcome.

Jack, the bastard, only chuckled again.

"You know, I didn't believe it before." He shrugged. "I tend to take what the tabloids say with a grain of salt, considering how much they stalk me and my company only to print lies in return. But looking at the two of you now, staring at the world-renowned bachelor of the century—well, second to me, of course—Ballard Dubois, with none other than my hand-me-down, Janelle Howerton, is nothing more than astonishing. You actually have some kind of appeal as a couple, on a very basic, very uninteresting level."

Ballard didn't tense. He didn't move and he didn't buckle under Jack's insults. What he did was something Janelle would cherish for the rest of her life.

"Then we'll bid you good-night, sir, and wish you all the best," Ballard said with a nod of his head. He turned then, moving Janelle along with him, and ushered her back into the hall without another word.

Jack, to her surprise, hadn't said another word either. She'd wanted to turn back to see the look on his face as they'd left him standing there alone but hadn't dared. Instead she reentered the room where music was once again playing and guests had either found themselves another drink or headed back to the dance floor for the last dances of the evening.

"Let's dance," Ballard said once they were inside.

Janelle thought about saying no. She thought about going around saying good-night and running the hell out of this hall to find the safety of her bedroom. But she didn't do that. What she did was look at Ballard, stared into his warm brown eyes and felt no danger, no scrutiny and no shame.

She nodded and followed him onto the dance floor.

In addition to the live and lovely vocal talents of Candice Glover, Janelle had also hired a DJ to play

special requests. For as high society as the Wintersage Academy alumni claimed to be, they all loved a
good line dance at their events. As they walked onto
the dance floor, she noticed the music had stopped
and she was about to turn to Ballard and suggest they
go instead. Then a song began to play, a song she remembered, and he pulled her into his arms. A rush
of heat, a feeling she was also growing familiar with,
washed over her.

The melodic piano interlude began and Ballard
started to sway. Janelle followed as the soulful sound
of Ruben Studdard singing "Unconditional" filtered
throughout the room. In that moment and the ones
to follow, nothing existed, nothing but her and Ballard. He stared down at her as they moved to the
music. In his gaze Janelle saw nothing but compassion and desire, simmering just beneath the surface
but there nonetheless. There were no questions, no
assumptions, no criticisms, just adoration, and her
heart filled. The words of the song fell around them,
cocooning them together as if the song were only
for them. She melted into him, leaning against the
strength of his embrace. When he leaned in closer to
kiss her forehead, Janelle could do nothing but close
her eyes to the sweetness, the security this man pro-
vided with his very presence, and the events of just
minutes ago dissolved. The memory, the shame—it
all washed away and ended when the song was complete.

# Chapter 9

"Jack and I were the perfect couple," Janelle said as she sat on the deep-cushioned sloped-back sage-green couch.

Ballard had asked her to spend the night with him and she'd agreed. Just like that. She hadn't thought about the implications, hadn't given herself a moment to wonder if it was the right decision or not. After they'd said their final good-nights at the hall and waited for the last of the vendors to vacate the building, she'd simply asked him to take her to her house, where she'd packed an overnight bag and left. Her father still wasn't home and she'd thought about leaving him a note but refrained. It had been almost a week since she'd seen him because he'd had more campaign stops to make throughout the state, and because she hadn't completed the task he'd asked of her, she hadn't really minded.

They'd arrived at Ballard's condo on the waterfront just after midnight. The hour-long drive had proceeded in silence as Ballard held Janelle's hand and she looked out the window at the passing night skyline. Once inside, he'd taken her bag and brought them each a glass of wine. Now they were sitting on his couch, which was strategically placed in the living room to face the ceiling-to-floor window that boasted a breathtaking view of Boston's waterfront.

"We dated all through college," she continued, cupping the half-full glass of wine with the palms of both hands. "My parents were ecstatic. His family felt the same way. Valentine's Day of our senior year, Jack proposed and I accepted. It was everything it was supposed to be—romantic and sweet and like a scene written in a novel. The next day it was in all the papers, local and international. My mother called me crying with joy and my father, of all people, began talking wedding dates."

She sighed, then sat back, taking a sip from her glass. "From that point on, everything we did or said was in the papers. Pictures were snapped as I walked from class to class or simply sat in the local pub for a drink with my friends. Our graduation was featured on some cable channel as a look into the simple life of rich and privileged college sweethearts."

Ballard sipped from his glass but otherwise remained perfectly still and quiet.

"Immediately following graduation we took our

first big trip together to Europe. Again we had paparazzi following us around as if they were on our personal payroll. About halfway through the trip, Jack began receiving business calls. For four days he had to travel back to the States while I stayed in Europe alone. When he returned, he was like another person entirely. He was distant and mean and we argued constantly."

Janelle sucked in a huge breath, released it slowly and let the worst admission of her life flow free.

"We'd had dinner at a restaurant. When we were finished, I wanted to go back to the room for some quiet time—since we'd managed to go an entire day without arguing. Jack wasn't ready to call it a night, so I went back alone. When he finally returned to the room, well after midnight, I was asleep. He'd come in, switching on the lights and yelling about feeling trapped, about not having any choices and finally about being stuck with me. He talked about our relationship, how he'd tried everything he knew to make things better but there was no hope. I don't think I'd been fully awake until that moment. Then I sat up in the bed and really looked at him. He was a stranger, just a shell of the man I thought I knew."

Exactly when Ballard had put his glass on the table, Janelle had no idea, but he leaned over, taking her glass from shaking fingers. Before she could clasp her hands together, he'd put her glass down on the table beside the couch and turned back to her, taking her hands in his hands, holding them tightly.

She bit back the sensation of choking, of being

strangled by this admission, and decided it was time to let it be free, decided that after all these years, this was the person she would admit the most embarrassing moment of her life to.

"He accused me of trying to trap him, of trying to marry into his family for their fortune. It didn't matter that my family was well off on its own. In Jack's mind his family was the elite. They were the top of the line and everyone else was beneath them, even me, I guess. He said some vile and awful things before he…" She paused, took a deep breath. "Before he tried to rape me."

Ballard's hands tightened around hers but he still did not speak.

"I fought back. I kicked and screamed and slapped at him. He backed off then and decided to use his words to assault me instead. I told him to leave and that I never wanted to see him again. He did and tonight was the first time I've seen him in person since.

"I didn't press charges. I didn't tell anyone what happened. I simply flew home. By that time Jack had already taken charge of the situation. His parents had called my parents to say that we'd decided it was too soon and that Jack needed to explore his options a little more before settling down. My father seemed disappointed, my mother sad but supportive of me. She encouraged me to find my own path, to figure out what I wanted to do and to just do it. Six months later I'd just begun to do that, had started my business and was talking with Sandra and Vicki about joining me, when I felt like I needed the business venture to be my fresh start. And that I couldn't have a fresh start without telling the people I loved most in the world the absolute truth. Before that could happen, my mother was killed in a car accident. My father went into a deep depression, my brother moved to New York and I threw myself into my business. I never thought about telling anyone again."

"Until tonight," Ballard finally said. "Until Jack Trellier showed up at the homecoming dance."

He spoke softly, as if he'd known this story all along and had simply waited for Janelle to actually speak the words. That wasn't possible, and yet his resignation, his quiet acceptance of everything she'd said, made her feel as if it wasn't so bad after all.

"I should have called the police while we were in Europe. I should have reported what he'd done instead of letting him brush our four-year relationship under the rug as if it were the most natural thing in the world. But I didn't," she said quietly. "I just didn't."

"He should have been put in jail," Ballard said, surprising her with the sting of his quietly spoken words. "Or at the very least he should have been beaten to within an inch of his miserable life. And you should have had peace for these past five years."

Janelle shook her head. "I can't go back. I can't retrace those steps and do the right thing."

"You can do the right thing now," he suggested.

She gave a wry chuckle. "In the midst of my father's campaign, just when the Silk Sisters are beginning to make a huge splash across the States and possibly internationally for Sandra." Shaking her head, she tried to dismiss his words, tried to push them out of her mind. "What's done is done," she told him. "There's no going back now. I'll look like a fool and everyone around me will suffer."

"And Jack will continue to taunt you."

Janelle pulled her hands from his. She stood and walked to the window, where she simply stared out into the night sky at the way the lights from surrounding buildings danced happily over the water.

"I'm not the person I was back then. I'm stronger, so he can't get to me. He tried tonight but I wouldn't let him. I stood up to him. I don't think he liked that but I don't care. I'm not going to rehash the past but I'm also not going to continue to let it dictate my future." She knew Ballard was listening attentively to her, but she somehow felt those words were more meant for her ears only. It was a declaration she'd needed to make, a step she'd needed to take, and she was proud that she had.

When Ballard came up behind her, slipping his hands around her waist and pulling her back against his rigid chest, she almost sighed. Leaning in close, he spoke directly into her ear.

"You're a remarkably resilient woman, Janelle. An exceptional female if I've ever met one."

That was not what she'd expected him to say, not exactly how she'd expected him to feel.

She turned then until she faced him, lifted her arms to wrap around his neck. When she looked up into his dark eyes, she realized this was exactly where she wanted to be. He was exactly who she needed at this moment in time.

"This remarkably resilient exceptional female would like for you to take her into your bedroom and to make love to her until the sun comes up. What are the chances of that happening?"

*The chances are overwhelmingly good,* Ballard almost replied. Instead he lowered his head until his lips lightly brushed over hers.

"There's nothing I wouldn't give you, Janelle. Nothing I wouldn't do to make you happy," he told her, his words a whisper over her mouth.

He could feel her letting go, sinking deeper into their embrace the same way she had when they'd been dancing. With a start, he realized how much he enjoyed that feeling, how good it was to have a woman such as Janelle leaning into him for support, for comfort. He was overwhelmed with that foreign sensation again, the one that had been steadily snaking its way around his heart like a chain.

"But I need you to be clear on this. I need you to be absolutely certain," he told her, exercising an amount of restraint he'd never known he had.

Her reply was a soft whimper, a barely heard "Thank you" just before her lips covered his, her tongue snaking along the line of his lips. Ballard opened his mouth. He let her inside, let the warmth of her tongue tangle with his. His hands flattened on her back, moved down lower to the small of her back, the curve before her buttocks, pressing her closer to him, to his burgeoning erection.

In the next instant he was lifting her into his arms. When she wrapped her legs around his waist, clasping her ankles to hold herself tighter against him, Ballard wanted to scream. For the first time in his life, the first time in all his dealings with females, he wanted to shout at the top of his voice, "Yes!" and they hadn't even made it to the bedroom yet.

That was easily remedied as he took two backward steps, then turned with his arms wrapped tightly around her, walking them down the hallway that led to the master bedroom.

His bed—dark oak, four-poster and king-size— lifted onto a platform in the middle of the room. He stopped at that point, laying her gently onto the forest-green comforter. He hated that their lips were no longer touching, their bodies no longer connected, and leaned down to suckle her tongue into his mouth one more time before finally pulling away.

Ballard's fingers moved nimbly over the buttons of her blouse as he removed it with slow, intentional movements. Next were her shoes, the sexy-as-hell heels he'd watched her walking on throughout the entire night. With powerful strokes, he rubbed the balls of her feet, her arch and then her heels. She moaned and his erection thickened, lengthening along his thigh. Her pants were slipped slowly down her legs, her stockings removed, and then she lay there clad in only her underwear. Ballard swallowed. Hard.

He looked down at the sheer perfection of her,

the milk-chocolate tone of her skin highlighted by the black-and-red panties and bra she wore. And he wanted like never before.

His clothes were removed in a more fevered fashion, his shoes and shirt going in one direction, pants, socks and boxers in another. When he climbed up onto the bed, it was to her open arms. As he rolled to the side, he pulled her with him, her palms flattening on his chest, then clasping his shoulders. Her leg lifted to wrap around his. Ballard grasped her thigh, pulled her leg up closer, higher, so that their bodies moved tighter together. His hand flattened over her thigh, traveling upward until the bare skin of her bottom was in his palm. He gripped tightly, his lips finding hers again.

Their kiss was hot and hungry, tongues, teeth, lips twining in an animalistic fashion as their hands fought for how much they could touch and how soon. When his fingers found the clasp of her bra, he twisted until the wisp of material fell and her breasts were free. Ballard pushed her back against the comforter, his lips moving from hers along the line of her jaw, down her neck and farther until he found the gems he was looking for. In one hand he cupped her full breast. With the other he plumped one breast so that the nipple was puckered and ready for the swipe of his tongue.

She arched her back and her breasts thrust farther into his face. He gorged himself on what should be declared a delicacy. After moments of giving all his attention to one breast, he switched places to the other, loving how she felt in his hands, how her skin tasted against his tongue. His mind was so full of her, the fresh, lightly perfumed scent of her skin, the sound of her voice, the sight of her smile. He couldn't get enough, couldn't stop until he had it all.

He pulled her panties down her legs, his chest heaving as he reached into his nightstand drawer to secure a condom. He ripped open the packet, saw her watching him intently, her eyes darkened with the same hunger he felt coursing through his body, and offered it to her.

Janelle accepted the packet, coming up on her knees and reaching down to touch his length. Her hands shook and she cursed.

Ballard touched her wrists, holding her still.

"You are beautiful and desirable and there's no other place I'd rather be right now. No other female I'd rather be with," he told her honestly.

She hadn't looked up at him while he spoke, hadn't commented, had actually not moved a muscle.

"Look at me, Janelle."

She didn't.

"Look at me." He spoke a little louder, waited a beat before applying a light jerk of her hands.

She looked up then, her bare shoulders squaring as if she was ready for whatever he was willing to give her, more words of adoration or, to his dismay, even some of abuse. That chain around his heart tightened and he clenched his teeth.

"I want to do this," she confessed. "I want to be with you and I want it to be good for both of us."

"Then you and I are all that matter right now. Understand?"

She nodded and gave a nervous smile that grew instantly to a look of pure passion as she moved her hands over his length, slipping the latex down over him, rubbing the pad of her thumb over his tip. Ballard remained still, focusing on the fall of her hair around her shoulders, the curve of her chin, the unsteady sound of her breathing. Anything but her fingers wrapped around him and the threat of losing himself right there in her hands.

When her lips touched his stomach, Ballard's eyes went wide. She kissed her way upward until she'd traced a hot path up to his pectorals. His hands went to her shoulders as he finally pushed her back so that he could take her lips once more. This time the kiss was a volatile transaction, one accompanied by the impatience of finally joining, finally becoming one.

Janelle lay back on the bed, spreading her legs for him, and Ballard thought he would weep with joy. Instead he clenched his teeth, kneeling between her. He lifted her legs, staring down at her offering, feeling the urge to simply dive in and explore. He owed her more than that, owed them both more than that. So he lifted her legs, let them fall over his shoulders as he lowered himself to her. With a whisper, just a breath away from plump vulva, he spoke her name.

She arched upward with an urgent "Yes."

His lips touched her then, felt the warmth of her essence against the softest of skin. Knowing one taste was never going to be enough, Ballard kissed up and down, suckling her into his mouth. When her hands grabbed the sides of his head, guiding him, leading him, encouraging him to take more, he did. With a finger, he spread her juicy lips to find the puckered nub of her center. He kissed her there, pulled the nub into his mouth and sucked until prerelease dripped from his tip into the safety of the latex.

She trembled then, went still and called out his name as her release rippled through her. Ballard loved the sound of his name in her voice. He loved the way she held on to him so tightly, as if she thought he might stop the delicious torture. He loved the way her arousal tasted against the back of his throat. And when he pulled back, placed the head of his engorged erection to the moistness of her opening, Ballard thought he might die if he didn't feel her wrapped securely, hotly, desperately around him.

Sliding into Janelle was a mixture of pleasure and pain—pleasure in that Ballard was sure he'd never felt anything as tight and as sweet as being buried deep inside her. Pain because he wanted to stay in this very spot forever but knew that was impossible.

She moved beneath him and they developed a rhythm that played out as beautifully as any classical arrangement. It was a slow and steady pace, an exploration of each other as he pulled out until only the tip was left inside, listened for her little gasp of need, then sank back into her waiting heat once more. He loved when her legs were draped over his shoulders, his depth so much more under his control. She liked when he switched places with her, allowing her to straddle him, to ride him into a complete state of oblivion that he barely escaped from. But he did escape, to pull her up on her knees and enter her from behind. There he held her with one arm wrapped around her stomach as he thrust in and out of her, both of them panting and moaning until she shivered with release and he followed with a guttural moan and a fierceness that he thought might be dangerous for them both.

"Stay with me," Ballard whispered after they'd showered and were back in his bed, still naked, blankets pulled up to cover them.

She chuckled. "You already asked that and I agreed. I even went home to get an overnight bag— don't you remember?"

"I remember," he replied, cuddling her closer to him because he felt as if she couldn't get close enough, he couldn't hold on tight enough. "What I meant to say was, stay with me this weekend. We can hang out here and do something neither of us gets enough time to do—relax. Then I'll see if I can convince Chef Javier to come and prepare us another scrumptious meal so we won't have to bother with going to a restaurant. On Sunday there's dinner at my grandparents', which I think you'll enjoy."

She stiffened for one split second. "I don't want to alter your plans. I can just rent a car and drive home tomorrow."

Ballard wasn't taking no for an answer, but if she wanted him to start trying to convince her, he'd gladly do so. He kissed her bare shoulder, lightly nipped the spot with his teeth and then licked over it. She moaned and he smiled.

"I want you to alter more than my plans," he admitted.

When she backed her bottom farther into his awakening arousal, Ballard smiled.

"How about we work on altering a few more positions right now and talk about tomorrow tomorrow," she suggested.

Lifting her leg to drape back over his own, Ballard let his hand slip between her legs, sighing when he found her wet and waiting.

"That sounds like an excellent plan," was his immediate reply. "Sounds like one hell of a plan."

# Chapter 10

As gorgeous as the view from Ballard's apartment was, Janelle didn't want to stay inside. Around noon, when he'd kept the television on the movie channels and put the newspaper in the trash can under his kitchen sink, she figured out what he was trying to do. And it was very sweet, but hiding had never been an option for her.

"Let's go see a movie," she said finally, getting up off the couch and going into the bedroom.

Ballard was dressed in baggy lounge pants drawn at his slim waist and a T-shirt that displayed every muscle from his perfectly sculpted shoulders to the vein-snaked arms and back to the bulge of his pectorals and his ripped abs. The shirt actually hid nothing and accentuated everything that made her mouth water if she stared at him too long.

"Are you sure? We could get movies on Netflix and order in. I've already been in touch with Javier and he said he'd be here around five to get dinner started."

Janelle had just taken a pair of jeans out of her bag and dropped them onto the bed. "I don't often get days off, Ballard. And I'm guessing the same goes for you. I want to do something fun, something I haven't done in a while. Besides, it's gorgeous outside today. Even a walk along the dock would be great."

"You know I'll do whatever you want," he told her, looking skeptical.

She nodded. "I know and I appreciate your efforts, but I'm not going to stay locked in here just so no one will snap another picture of us and print it. I'm not going to let them win."

"Is that what you were afraid of? Pictures of us in the paper?"

"Not afraid. Annoyed. I don't like all that exposure but I know now it's inevitable," she replied. "So grab some clothes. We'll get a shower and head out for the day."

The shower lasted longer than either of them anticipated, as about midway through, she'd dropped the soap onto the tiled floor. Bending over to pick it up, Janelle felt Ballard's hand on her bottom. He rubbed there with soapy hands smoothing over her skin, his slick fingers slipping through the crevice to tease and taunt. She attempted to stand up straight but was held in place by his palm to the small of her back. His fingers continued to move, slipping farther between her legs until he found her core, then delving inside. Plastering her palms on the tiled walls, Janelle sucked in a breath and he penetrated her, moving two fingers in and out of her. His other hand found its way around to cup her breast and his teasing continued until she could barely breathe, could barely keep her eyes open. Water pounded onto her back as Ballard continued to move in and out of her. She wanted to call his name, to tell him the plan was to go out, but the words did not come, only gasps of pleasure.

When both his hands went to her waist and then to her bottom, separating her cheeks so that the warm water could stream down and drip from between her legs with her essence, she trembled. Next his erection slipped between her cheeks, the head of his arousal pressing persistently until gliding into her waiting heat. She sucked in a breath and he began to move, pounding into her with almost the same rhythm as the shower water.

Never in her limited sexual experience had Janelle felt this wanton, this uninhibited, with a man. Even last night she'd been afraid of not pleasing Ballard, of not giving him an experience on the level he was used to. She knew he'd been with many women and had most likely experienced much more than she ever had. Janelle had had only two other lovers, including Jack, and neither had been worth writing about.

Ballard's hand came around to toy with the tight nub of her center while he continued to pump into

A.C. Arthur                              133

her and she thought she would lose her mind, the
sensations rippling through her were so intense. She
wanted to scream with pleasure, yell her release to the
entire world. More so, however, she wanted to give
Ballard some of the same pleasure she was receiving.

It was a good thing that Ballard's bathroom was
big enough to accommodate a Little League team, his
shower stall probably able to fit six people if needed.
She moved away from him quickly so he wouldn't
reach for her and turned to see him looking half-
dazed at her departure. When he opened his mouth
to speak, she moved into him, touching a finger to
his lips and making a shushing sound. He closed his
lips and she kissed them. She smiled as her next kiss
landed on his cheek, then the other cheek, then his
chest. Both pectorals and down to his abs, which
looked as if they should definitely be photographed
and admired on a daily basis. She went lower still,
her heart racing with anticipation.

His arousal was hard and long and thick and a little
intimidating as she faced it. But when she wrapped
her hand around him and heard his quick intake of
breath, she grew bolder. She had both hands around
him then, one sliding to the tip of his length while
the other stayed grounded at the base, two fingers
slipping beneath to tweak his balls. Ballard leaned
against the wall then, his breathing definitely faster,
more labored. Prerelease oozed from the tip and
Janelle dipped her head to sample. She pulled back,
dipped her head again and had the entire bulbous head
of him in her mouth to suckle. Minutes later she was

still on her knees, Ballard's fingers digging into her shoulders before he finally pulled away.

He ground out the words "Come here," and lifted her into his arms.

She dutifully wrapped her legs around his waist, sliding down over his length. He turned again so that her back was against the wall and worked her until they both were out of breath, both moaning and gasping as their releases hit simultaneously, almost knocking them down completely.

Another first, Ballard thought as he escorted Janelle through the honey-oak front doors of the senior Dubois estate. He could have sent her home, or rather, let her go home to Wintersage yesterday or earlier this morning, for that matter. He could have simply not invited her to his place Friday night after the dance.

Ballard didn't even want to think about not having made the choices he had. He didn't want to think about the past forty-something hours that he'd had with her. The private time they'd shared in his place, in his bed, his shower, his arms. The conversations that had pulled them closer together, that made him understand and admire the woman she was so much more. He would have had none of that had he stuck to his normal dating ritual and had she stuck to her no-dating ritual.

In that respect he was glad for change.

Walking through the house he'd loved as a child to the family room with its three couches, full-service bar, French doors and terrace that wrapped around a good portion of the side of the house, he felt proud and pleased at the same time. He felt good about bringing her here and about what this action meant. What Ballard would not allow himself to feel was curiosity. He wouldn't ask himself why—why her? Why now? He would not wonder at what all this really meant. He couldn't afford to.

"This is a beautiful home," she was saying from beside him.

He guided her to the couch. "I loved coming to visit when I was young. Pops used to have this butler named Oz."

Ballard moved to the other side of the room, where the bar was located, as he continued talking, taking down two glasses and going to the small refrigerator to pull out two bottled waters.

"He was as wide as a door and so tall I used to call him a giant. He was from the West Indies and had this great accent. We'd play hide-and-seek and he'd take forever to find me even though I think he knew where I was all along." Ballard chuckled at the memory.

"Sounds like fun. DJ and I played hide-and-seek until the day when I was ten and he locked me in the closet I hid in instead of coming to find me. I was in there for at least an hour before I realized he wasn't coming to get me and that he'd locked the door. My dad was livid. I thought he was going to kill DJ."

This time Ballard tossed his head back, he laughed so hard. That was another thing he'd done a lot of this weekend. He'd laughed and relaxed and thought of other things besides work. They'd gone to the movies to see something he would have never thought to see in a movie theater on his own or to rent and watch alone. Superheroes weren't his thing but Janelle had been adamant about seeing the new Thor installment and even more over-the-top excited as the movie progressed and one of her favorite actors, Idris Elba, made his screen appearance. He'd been happy that she was happy and slightly jealous at the obvious affection she had for the movie star.

Now he was laughing with her again, being comfortable and at home with a female he'd met only about a month ago.

"Nora told me you had someone with you," Leandra said, coming into the room, her cream-colored skirt sparkling with the same floral design as the matching jacket she wore.

She looked from her grandson to the woman sitting on the couch and her smile almost touched from one ear to the other. As for Ballard, his hand tightened on the glass he held.

"Hello," Janelle was saying as she stood and took a step forward to greet Leandra, who had moved across the room faster than Ballard had seen her move in quite some time. "I'm Janelle Howerton and you have a gorgeous home, Mrs. Dubois."

Leandra clasped Janelle's outstretched hand, cradling it in both of her weathered ones.

"And you are pretty as a picture. Look at that smile, Ballard. She's lovely. Here, sit back down, Janelle, and let me get to know you better."

Ballard still stood at the bar, lifting his glass to his lips for a gulp. The hand that clapped his shoulder had him just about to choke because he knew who it was and what was about to be said.

"Good job, son, good job," Hudson whispered to him, which was unnecessary, because across the room his grandmother had Janelle totally engaged in another conversation. "She's prettier in person than her pictures. And she's polite. Your grandmother likes her already."

"Of course she's polite, Pops. She's a lady."

"Yes. Yes, she's a lady. From a good family. Her father's got a good shot at winning that seat." Hudson moved around where Ballard stood, fixing his own drink, Hennessy, as always.

"He's looking for our support," Ballard said, remembering Janelle's email that he'd never responded to.

"And he should get it. His platform's solid, his business is booming and we might just end up being family. Your father's met him, too, said he's a good man who lost his wife some time back. Yeah, we should talk about what we can do for Howerton's campaign and how long I'll have to wait for you and that pretty one over there to make things official."

"There's nothing to make official, Pops. We just met not too long ago, so we're just trying to get to know each other."

"All you need to know is that she's the one," Hudson said before taking a swallow of his drink. When he put the glass down on the marble-top surface, he looked over to where Leandra and Janelle sat, then back to Ballard. "If it feels right, if you can't sleep without dreaming of her, can't breathe without smelling her scent, I don't care when you met her, she's the one."

Throughout dinner, after having introduced Janelle to his father and his grandfather, Ballard thought of Hudson's words. He thought of the impressions they'd put in his mind as the conversation buzzed around them. Leandra and Janelle talked about Europe and he didn't miss the slight edge to her voice throughout that exchange. She hadn't had a good time while she'd been there. His fists balled in his lap as he thought of why. If he weren't the businessman, the face of Dubois Maritime, he would have beat the hell out of Jack Trellier Friday night as he'd stood in that hallway insulting Janelle as if she'd actually deserved to be faced with him again after all he'd put her through.

Instead he'd opted to get Janelle out of there before all his reservations were dismissed and he did what his gut told him he should. As he'd thought it would be, yesterday's tabloids had featured an old picture of Trellier and Janelle, then another more current one with Ballard and Janelle leaving Area Four hand in hand. The headline had been High-Society Love Triangle. He'd gone into his home office and shredded the paper immediately, before Janelle could see it. His fingers flexed as once again he thought about punching that jerk Trellier.

"I'd like to speak with you, son," Daniel said in a

hushed tone across the table so the others wouldn't hear him.

Ballard hid the frown that threatened to appear. He wasn't in the mood for his father right now, not in the mood to be questioned about the Chan deal or the new offices in New York or anything else, for that matter. All Ballard wanted to do was cherish the time he had left with Janelle. When they left here, he'd be taking her back to her home in Wintersage and probably wouldn't see her for the rest of the week, as his schedule was pretty full for the next few days.

"We're about to have dessert," he replied, not at all interested in the lemon meringue pie his grandfather had already mentioned at least three times throughout the meal.

"We'll skip it. This is more important," Daniel insisted, dropping his napkin onto his plate and standing.

Ballard doubted that but he wasn't about to embarrass his father or draw any more of his grandfather's attention by remaining in his seat. So he stood and when Janelle turned to look up at him, he went on impulse alone. Bending down, he kissed her forehead and whispered, "Be right back."

She smiled up at him, then turned back to his grandmother, whose eyes simply glowed with knowledge.

He followed his father back to the den, and Daniel stood in front of one of his grandmother's French-inspired sofas.

"Chan's not signed," was Daniel's first comment.

"He will be," Ballard replied.

"You said that last week and it's still not done."

"He's not the only candidate for this contract, Dad. I'm not about to cave on his terms just because he likes to think so. Now, I'm confident he will come around." Ballard slipped a hand into his pant pocket. He'd worn jeans today, dark denim, and a white button-down shirt. He couldn't remember the last time he'd worn jeans, but when Janelle had pulled another pair out of her bag this morning, sliding her long legs into the denim, then topping them off with high-heeled boots, he'd figured that was the style of the day and mimicked her attire. Before leaving his apartment, he'd grabbed her close, using his cell phone to take an impulsive selfie of them. They'd giggled all the way down to the car and she'd insisted he text her the picture so she'd have it on her phone, as well. He almost smiled at the memory but knew that would only tick his father off more.

"You must remain focused, Ballard. There's no time for this dalliance you're involved in now. The press is distracting," Daniel insisted.

His father was an inch or so taller than Ballard, his build still muscled even if he'd lost about ten pounds since the divorce. He was dressed in a casual suit of dark brown slacks and a dark-brown-and-black-checked jacket. His dress shirt was unbuttoned at the collar but Ballard was sure there was a tie in the glove compartment of his father's car just in case he had to do some business.

"Was Mother distracting?" Ballard asked impulsively. "Was being married to her and having a child too distracting for you to give us your attention?"

The question had burned in Ballard's mind since the day he'd left for college. Over the years he'd convinced himself that it didn't matter, that it was done. His father was who he wanted to be and, as such, he was in exactly the position he wanted to be in.

Daniel didn't move but for the tick of muscle in his jaw. "What did you say to me?"

"I asked you a question," Ballard insisted. "I asked you if business was really the most important thing in your life. Did you really prefer to close a deal rather than spend the weekend with your wife, with your son?"

"You have no right," Daniel began.

"I have every right!" Ballard yelled back. "You made a commitment to us, too, and you let us down so you could run your business. Now you stand here daring to give me that same stupid-ass advice. Well, I don't need your advice now. Those days have long passed and you missed that boat."

He paused, clenching his teeth and thinking that maybe he should walk away. Maybe he should let the rush of emotion pounding through his chest go and move on. But he couldn't, not now that he'd begun.

"I've done that for years," Ballard continued, "and probably missed out on more living than I'll ever manage to get back. But no more, Dad. I'm not going that route anymore. I'll get Chan to sign the contracts and if not, I'll get someone else. I know how to do my job. But I also know how to handle my personal business."

He did leave then, because seeing the look of pure fury on his father's face told him that all his words had only scratched against the ego of the great Daniel Dubois. They hadn't pricked the skin of the man, hadn't made him feel one ounce of guilt or regret. So his words didn't matter, not to his father, anyway.

To Ballard, though, they had and he headed back into the dining room to finish the dinner he'd been enjoying with his grandparents and the woman he couldn't seem to have enough of. When Hudson lifted his glass for a toast after they'd finished their pie, Ballard lifted his, as well, watching with a smile on his face as Janelle and his grandmother joined in.

"To Ballard and Janelle, a cuter couple I've never seen," Hudson began until Leandra cleared her throat. "Oh, ah, well, I guess I have seen a cuter couple, about fifty-some-odd years ago," he corrected with a wink to his wife.

When Leandra smiled, Ballard put his free arm around Janelle's shoulders, loving once more the way she leaned into him.

"May you both achieve all your dreams and love like there's no tomorrow," Hudson finished.

They sipped from their glasses and Ballard tried not to notice Janelle had stiffened at his grandfather's mention of the word *love*.

# *Chapter 11*

Chan finally signed the deal and Ballard scanned the signed contracts, then emailed them to his father and grandfather. Afterward he sat back in his leather office chair, rubbing a hand over his goatee, thinking about all that he'd accomplished and all that his father lacked.

Daniel Dubois needed to take a break. He needed to go to some island and find a beautiful woman. He needed to feel that rush of male blood coursing through his veins again, to smell the ocean, watch the sunrise and sunset and live again. And Ballard could run the company while his father recovered.

All he had to do was marry Janelle.

He pushed that idea right out of his mind as fast as it appeared there. Marriage was not on his radar.

Even in light of the speech he'd just given his father, it simply wasn't for him. He'd never thought about that type of commitment, never wanted to be that beholden to a female. And if he were really honest with himself, outside of the fact that it was Monday and he was missing her since they'd spent the entire weekend together, he still didn't think he had what his grandfather did. It was that something special a person had when they found another person that enabled them to stick it out through the good and bad, to stay in a marriage and make it the happiest union ever.

His father apparently didn't have it, so Ballard wasn't surprised when those feelings didn't move through him either. It was just the way it had to be with them both, he figured.

As the afternoon dragged on, when he still couldn't get thoughts of her out of his head and his grandfather's voice echoed in the back of his mind, Ballard shut his computer down and packed up his things. For the first time in he didn't know how long, he was leaving the office early. He wasn't going to run home and change and hit the road to go and visit Janelle—he'd already decided it was too soon to do something that drastic. Besides, he could go a day without seeing her. His grandfather's words had been fanciful and spoken by an old man who had been married most of his life. Of course he thought his wife was the star, the sun, the moon. That was the way he should think.

Ballard needed to think differently, but he still needed to get the hell out of this office for the rest of the day.

* * *

"You spent the entire weekend with Ballard Dubois and you want us to believe that absolutely nothing happened," Vicki said as the threesome sat in their favorite seat near the window at the Quarterdeck.

"I didn't say absolutely nothing," Janelle replied, attempting to hide a smile but not being very successful.

Her mood had been almost giddy since arriving home last night. The weekend had been unexpected and almost surreal. She hadn't spent time sleeping in the same bed with a man since she'd been in Europe. In fact, she hadn't even entertained the notion since she'd given up on dating altogether. Yet when he'd asked her to go with him, she'd followed and she hadn't regretted one moment of that decision.

"All right, then spill," Sandra said, sitting back to accept the plate of food the waitress had just set in front of her.

They all took a few moments to bless their food before the attention was once again front and center on Janelle.

"Okay, look, I want to first say that this was not a part of the plan. I invited him to the dance and then he invited me to Boston for the weekend. It was very impromptu."

"Uh-huh, and was it also very good?" Sandra asked.

Vicki smiled. "You're practically glowing, so I'm going to guess that answer is yes."

Janelle chewed on a French fry until it was gone,

then nodded. "It was very good. Better than I re-membered."

"That's because your memory was of Jack," Sandra told her. "Can you believe all that nonsense he's been feeding reporters since the dance?"

"Disgusting. He should have stayed wherever he's been hiding himself all these years," Vicki chimed in. "I couldn't believe when I saw him waltz into that dance as if he'd lived here all his life. And as if he'd been invited here in the first place. Arrogant bastard!"

Janelle had been about to pick up another fry, happy to be chatting with her girlfriends about the guy she was just a little bit crazy about. So their shift in conversation was more than a little surprising.

"Wait, what are you talking about? What has Jack been doing since Friday?" she asked them.

Sandra and Vicki exchanged a look.

"What, have you been under a rock? I know we don't make a habit of reading the tabloids, but national papers even picked up that story from yesterday, especially with all the election talk mentioned in it."

Election talk? What the hell?

"No, I haven't been under a rock. Ballard and I just spent the weekend focusing on each other, not work and not anything to do with work." She'd noted that as she'd awakened this morning and walked into the kitchen to make coffee.

Her father had left her a note saying he had a meeting in Boston this morning and that he wanted to talk to her the moment he arrived home around seven this evening. It probably also explained why Ballard had been so intent on keeping her inside his condo at all costs.

"So you haven't seen any of the newspapers or tabloids?" Sandra asked. She'd put down her wine-glass and was now looking at Janelle with concern.

"No. Should I have?"

"Oh, sweetie," Vicki began.

Janelle held up a hand. "No. Just tell me what they said." She didn't want the pitiful looks or the sorrow-ful tone. Whatever was going on, she wanted to deal with it head-on, not through blurry eyes.

"Jack's bringing up your past relationship. In one article he says he thinks you may be the one that got away. In another one he's making accusations that this thing with you and Ballard isn't serious at all, that it's just a front for the political joining of Dubois and your dad," Vicki told her.

Sandra nodded. "That's the first one I saw because Jordan was on the phone with Windom about it when we were supposed to be having a family dinner."

"No," Janelle whispered. "Why would he do that? Why would he come all the way back here and stir up this type of trouble?"

"Maybe he is feeling like he missed out with you. Maybe he's regretting calling off the wedding," Vicki suggested.

"He didn't call off the wedding—I did!" Janelle yelled back. "And he's lucky that's all I did after his antics at the château that night."

Both Sandra and Vicki grew quiet and Janelle sat back in her seat. She was fuming, the tips of her ears stinging, she was so angry. Her heart beat a rapid rhythm at the thought of what Ballard must have thought when he saw those articles, because she had no doubt he had seen them.

"What antics?" Sandra asked.

"When you came back, you said you broke up, that he decided he wasn't ready. Then you went into the dating hibernation," Vicki added.

Janelle debated for another second or so if she should tell them or not. It was in the past—why couldn't it just stay there? Obviously, Jack wasn't respecting the past aspect, so why should she? Why had she all those years ago?

Appetite gone, Janelle pushed the plate away from her and totally ignored her drink. "He was drunk," she began, then paused. "No, I don't think he was drunk at all. He came into the room saying all sorts of crazy stuff about me not pleasing him and being too frigid for him. Then he tried to rape me."

She'd said it. For the second time in just four days she'd admitted what had happened after holding silent for five years. She took a deep breath and actually shrugged this time.

"I don't know why I didn't tell you before. No, I do. I was ashamed. Embarrassed by what I thought at the time was the perfect relationship. We'd been together for years and while everyone else was breaking up or having trouble with cheating boyfriends, I had Jack and he'd been perfect. My parents liked him because they were certain he didn't want me for my money, since his family had enough of their own.

We were going to be a great power couple as they'd said. Then it was over."

"Okay." Sandra spoke first. "I'm going to be upset with you for not confiding in us then, but that will happen later. Right now I want to know when you plan to call the police and report that asshole for what he did to you."

She shook her head, her temples throbbing with the building headache. "I had no plans of ever telling anyone. He went his way and I went mine. Now, actually, right after that night, I realized that was the best thing to ever happen to me."

"Really, Janelle? He almost raped you and you say it's the best thing that ever happened to you?" Sandra was very upset.

Janelle had known this was how it would go when she told them. Vicki looked as if she wanted to cry but Janelle just felt relief. It was out. To the most important people in her life the sordid story was out.

"I didn't tell before, because I didn't want to embarrass my family. And then when I'd finally gathered the courage to say something to my mother, she was killed. I let the secret be buried with her," Janelle told them. "I know I probably should have pressed charges, but we were engaged. It had been in all the papers and everyone in Wintersage was looking forward to what they were calling the wedding of the century. I just didn't want to let everyone down."

"Oh, honey," Vicki said, getting up from her seat and coming around to the side of the table where

Janelle sat to hug her. "I'm so sorry that happened to you. So sorry you thought you couldn't tell us."

Sandra looked as if she was ready to take out her cell phone and dial the police herself. Instead she extended her hand across the table and Janelle took it, clasping her fingers tightly with those of a woman she'd always considered a sister.

"So now we really need to put a stop to his media madness," Sandra said, taking a deep breath and releasing it slowly.

Janelle blinked back her own tears, smiling up at Vicki. "It will die down soon. Nobody really cares who I date."

"They do if getting the Dubois family to back your father ends up making him win the election. Windom's campaign is going to have a field day with that info. I'm surprised they haven't already started a counter attack," Vicki told her.

They both looked at Sandra, who shrugged. "I don't know. Jordan doesn't talk to me about it, because of my relationship with you. My parents are sort of taking the same stance and not talking about the election with either of us."

"Then I should go home and talk to my dad," Janelle announced.

"Are you going to tell him about what Jack did?" Vicki asked, whispering as if she didn't want anyone else to overhear her question even though she hadn't said anything bad.

"I'm going to tell him that I've tried to speak to

Ballard about the election and that I have no idea why Jack is back in the picture."

"You sure that's the right thing to do? This election is pretty important to him. If the details about what happened between you and Jack come out, it could hurt his chances," Sandra proposed.

Janelle had actually thought about this over the weekend. She'd thought about telling her father simply to clear her conscience, not realizing that it might somehow circle back to his campaign. But she was almost positive the last thing Jack Trellier wanted was for some bad press to destroy the company he'd worked so hard to obtain. This story would not bode well for Trell Cosmetics. Women internationally would be outraged at the thought that he would do something so vicious and just walk away. No, he didn't want it coming out. He simply wanted to irritate her, to see if she'd crack, if she'd either stop seeing Ballard or come crawling back to him. Neither of which was an option for her.

"I'm not telling my father if I don't absolutely have to. He's endured enough hurt," Janelle told them, knowing they probably still didn't approve of her decision.

Vicki nodded. "Besides, he'd probably kill Jack and then he'd never get elected."

"You've got that right," Sandra said. "I remember when we first started looking at boys, how Mr. Howerton and your brother used to watch us like a hawk when we were at your house. I don't suspect your father's temper and his protectiveness over you has ceased over the years, especially now that your mom's gone."

Janelle believed every word Sandra had just said. Her father—and brother—wouldn't take news of what had really happened in Europe well. All the more reason she would keep her mouth shut. Again.

Darren Howerton was sitting at the kitchen table dipping his spoon into a bowlful of chocolate chip ice cream when Janelle walked in.

"Great dinner selection," she said, going around behind him and leaning down to kiss him on the cheek.

"It's comfort food," was his reply. "That's what your mother used to say. Grab a spoon and have a seat." He nodded to the chair beside him.

As she'd already known this conversation was coming, Janelle did exactly as her father obliged. She'd had a hell of a day, with Everley adding to the guest count for her wedding and all the calls from the parents on the committee for the homecoming dance. She'd ignored those calls, hoping they had no idea she was actually back in town. Janelle had wondered why they were pestering her after the event had been a rousing success. Now, after talking to Sandra and Vicki and after stopping by her office to pull up the online versions of as many newspapers and tabloids as she could find from over the weekend, she knew exactly what the women wanted. More gossip.

She sat down and dipped her spoon into the side of the ice cream, put it in her mouth and licked it clean.

Her father chuckled. "You can still do that without getting brain freeze. Your brother would groan at the sight."

Janelle smiled, too. DJ never could eat his ice cream as fast as she could. He had brain freeze if he sipped from a straw too quickly.

"I miss him around the house," she admitted.

Her father nodded. "I miss him and your mom around the house."

They ate a little more in silence.

"I asked you to talk to Ballard Dubois about the election, not to get romantically involved with him," he said.

This wasn't quite what she thought her father would talk about, but she was okay addressing this subject, as well.

"I didn't want to go out with him at all. But I wanted to help you, to repay you for all the things you've done for me. The romance, well, that just sort of happened on its own."

Darren nodded. "I see. And what about Jack Trellier? He's just back in the picture on his own or did something else happen in that area, as well?"

"No," Janelle said adamantly. "Nothing happened in that area. Nothing at all. Jack showed up at the dance. He said because he'd seen the pictures in the paper of me and Ballard. I told him to get lost."

"And he began going to the papers on his own?"

"It looks that way."

"That boy's an ass," her father replied, his face

grim. "I'll reach out to his father and see what's what."

"No," Janelle said, quickly grasping her father's arm. "Just stay out of it. Please, Daddy. Your focus should be on the election. I've already talked to Ballard about your campaign and I met his family over the weekend. His grandfather seems fond of you and your candidacy, so I'm sure that's going to come through. Let me handle Jack, please."

Darren stared at her for what seemed like a million seconds. She wanted to squirm in her chair the way she used to as a kid and teenager when he'd stare at her that way. But she didn't. She was an adult and she was dealing with adult issues. Her father wanted to win this election, so she wanted that for him. As for Jack, Janelle wasn't entirely sure what he wanted, but what he was going to find out was that she was no longer the naive and impressionable young girl he'd once dated. And if he persisted with these stories, he was going to hate that fact now more than ever.

# Chapter 12

Days passed and none of them got any better. The stories continued to turn up in the papers. *TMZ* had even managed to catch Jack coming out of his Miami mansion and questioned him before he climbed into his red Lamborghini.

"First loves never die—you know that," he replied, looking straight into the camera, one of his brows lifted, his mouth stretched into the sexy smile that had long graced ads for the men's product line of Trell Cosmetics.

Janelle wanted to throw something at her television when she lay in her bed watching the eleven-o'clock news on Thursday night. Instead she picked up the remote control and pressed her finger so hard into the power button she thought it would break. The second the television snapped off, her cell phone vibrated on her nightstand, the screen lighting up the dark room. Rolling across the bed, she reached for the phone.

"Hello," she sighed, falling back against the pillows.

"He's an ass," the voice stated, and she smiled.

"I know. He's a gigantic ass who probably wears the makeup he sells."

Ballard chuckled. Janelle had become accustomed to hearing that sound. In fact, this week she'd become accustomed to his late-night phone calls. In the morning she would rise between ten and fifteen minutes later than usual as she tried to catch up on the sleep lost from talking to him well into the night. But there was nothing, not even seeing Jack Trellier's lying face on the television only seconds ago, that would keep her from answering the phone.

"He probably does," he continued. "So let's stop thinking about him."

Janelle sighed, lifting her free arm to let it drop over her forehead. "I don't think he's going to stop, Ballard. It's been almost a week and every day there's something else. It's like he's taunting me every second of every day."

"Think about this instead," Ballard suggested. "I could give you a massage, hot oil, candles, the works. All you'd have to do is lie there and accept the pleasure. My hands working out the kinks and all the stress from the week. I would rub you from head to toe, not missing a spot, taking care to make you moan every step of the way."

She felt herself sinking even farther into her mattress, the pillow cushioning her head, her fingers trembling slightly but not releasing the phone.

"Mmm, are you trying to talk dirty to me, Mr. Dubois?" she asked, unable to keep the smile from spreading across her face.

"I'm making you a proposition, Ms. Howerton."

"Well, then," she sighed, "please continue."

"Before the massage I'd run you a hot bubble bath. I'd undress you because you've had a very long and stressful day. I don't want you to strain yourself any further. I'd carry you to the tub and set you down ever so gently."

"Would you bathe me, too?" she asked, her arm slipping from her forehead to fall against the lower part of her belly, her fingers clenching the sheet that covered her.

"Oh, yes, you know I would," was his ready reply. "With slow and soft strokes, I'd rub the soapy sponge over your body, every inch of your body, because I don't want to miss any spots."

"No," she said, her voice all but a moan. "I wouldn't want you to miss a spot."

"I miss you, Janelle," he said seriously, suddenly.

Still wrapped in the haze of his soft voice, the thought of him actually bathing her, touching her, soothing her, Janelle tingled all over, his words like icing on the already-delicious cake. But she didn't know how to respond. No man had ever told her he missed her before. She wondered how she should feel to be missed.

"I need to see you," were his next words, continued as easily as if he were again talking about massaging her.

"It's almost midnight," she said clumsily.

"I have a car."

"A very nice car, I remember." She gripped the sheet even tighter.

"I could be there in thirty minutes."

She blinked. "It's an hour-long drive from your house."

"Not this time," he told her. "I'm in a hurry."

*What now?* she thought. The massage and bath talk had been soothing, arousing, but it had been talk and she'd figured that was where it would stop. Now he was suggesting coming here, tonight. And what was her protest to that?

"I'll be waiting," she said before she lost her nerve. "I'll be at the door waiting."

"Thirty minutes and, Janelle?"

"Yes," she answered breathily.

"Don't get dressed."

Twenty-eight minutes later she saw the headlights of Ballard's SUV pull up the driveway and she opened the front door. Fifteen minutes ago when she'd convinced herself that this was actually happening—she was waiting up for a man and a booty call—she'd come downstairs and disengaged the alarm system so her father wouldn't hear the door opening and closing.

She stood there in the open doorway, her hands shaking as she watched him step out of the SUV and walk toward the house. His gaze was locked on hers. She couldn't tear her eyes away. He was still wearing a suit, his tie loosened at his neck, his jacket open, swaying as he walked. When he stepped up onto the porch, Janelle licked her lips.

"You did as I asked," he said, stepping up to her, one hand instantly going behind her head, fingers curling into her hair as he pulled her closer. "Thank you."

She hadn't changed her clothes but stood at the door dressed in the nightgown she'd donned for sleep. Only the second his lips touched hers she knew that sleep was the last thing she'd be getting in the near future.

He'd thought about her all day. There hadn't been one second that Ballard had closed his eyes today that he hadn't seen her face, one moment that he couldn't hear her voice playing over and over again in his mind. She was saying his name, laughing at something he said, commenting on something they were doing. When he had lunch with two of the board members, he couldn't remember what they were saying from one moment to the next, couldn't keep track of the conversation or even manage to swallow his food without thinking about her.

It had been like an undiagnosed sickness throughout this entire week. The more he'd tried to push the thoughts and emotions away, the more they'd amplified. He'd stayed away on purpose, only calling her instead of suggesting they see each other. She'd seemingly obliged his need by working just as hard as he had and not requesting they see each other. But the need hadn't subsided. The desire to simply be near her had not ceased.

And so here he was. And there she was, standing in that doorway with that black-and-pink nightgown barely scraping her midthigh. The straps at her shoulders were thin, barely there. The material covering her breasts looked soft. Her nipples looked hard. *Hard* being a very operative word at this point. He'd kissed her because he hadn't been able to stop himself. He wouldn't make love to her here in the foyer of her father's home, but he would be inside her, soon. Or he'd die trying.

Dragging his lips away from hers was a struggle and they scraped over the side of her jaw as he asked, "Which way is your bedroom?"

She seemed dazed for a moment, then finally replied, "I have the west wing of the house to myself since DJ moved out."

"Great," Ballard breathed. With one arm still wrapped around her, he used the other to shut the front door. "Alarm?"

She nodded and took backward steps until she was standing near the control pad. He moved with her, not willing to relinquish his hold on her, and kissed her neck while he heard her pressing buttons.

When she finished and her hands came to rest at both sides of his face, Ballard simply stared into her eyes. For endless seconds they stood in that foyer staring, communicating on a level Ballard had never experienced before. She wanted him just as much as he wanted her. She missed him—he could tell by the way her grip on his face softened as her body pressed into his. Ballard could also swear he'd seen something else, a quick glimpse that had him catching his breath.

"Come with me," she whispered, and the momentary haze was broken.

She pulled away from him, taking his hand, and led him through the foyer all the way to the end, past the grand spiral staircase, through another doorway and a more basic-looking set of stairs to their left. They moved through the quiet house in silence, down another long hallway on the second floor and finally passed through the door to her room. Once inside, Janelle moved around him and clicked the lock on her bedroom door into place.

He was just about to remove his jacket when she appeared by his side. "Let me this time," she said softly, her hands going beneath his lapels, flattening with a circle of heat on his chest. She pushed the jacket from his shoulders and it fell to the floor.

Her room was very spacious, with her king-size bed flanked by nightstands, a huge painted portrait above. Across the room were a wall-mounted flat-screen television and two bureaus. Straight ahead, just to the left of closed balcony doors, was a lounge chair. That was all he could see from where he stood and in the dim light of one of the lamps on the night-stand. But none of that really interested him anyway.

Ballard looked down, watching Janelle's mani-cured nails as she pulled his shirt from his pants and unbuttoned each button. When that fell to the floor beside his jacket, she lifted his tank over his head and once again ran her palms along the breadth of his chest. He'd missed this feeling, this elation at her touch, missed it more than he could dare to explain.

When her hands went to his buckle, her fingers grazing his length as she unzipped his pants, he sucked in a breath. His shoes were easy and he stepped out of them as she pushed his pants and boxers over his hips and down his legs. He was naked now, standing in front of her, exposed and aroused. She looked at him just as though it were the first time before reaching out to take his hand again. He realized in that moment that he really liked being led around by her.

Before she climbed onto her bed, she pulled her nightgown over her head, tossing it to the floor, revealing the fact that she'd been naked beneath. His fingers curled with the need to touch her, to wrap around the span of her waist and hold her still while he pounded into her. She surprised him yet again when she went to her nightstand and pulled out her own box of condoms.

"Prepared, are we?" he asked, his tone not as joking as he would have liked because his interminable erection was quite possibly stopping all blood flow to his brain.

She shrugged. "I just bought them on Monday. Figured after the weekend they might actually come in handy now. And look here, just a few days later."

Janelle smiled as she ripped open the package. Ballard smiled with her, stepping close to the bed while she sheathed him. That moment was officially the end of the waiting game for him and he eased her down on the bed, propped her legs up onto his shoulders and slipped happily into the most wonderful place on earth…and quite possibly in the heavens, too.

It was like coming home after a long day at work, sitting on the couch and slipping off his shoes, sipping a glass of wine and sighing with relief. No, Ballard thought as he pulled out and sank back in, it was better.

"So good," he whispered as he moved.

"Yes. So damned good," she replied, her fingers gripping the blankets beneath her.

He loved being on top of her, looking down into her pleasure-riddled face, hearing her gasps. From this position he could also watch her breasts moving along with the rhythm and continue to be aroused. She was so sexy, so alluring and so exciting. From their lengthy phone conversations to their dinner dates, she was absolutely perfect in every way he could imagine.

She didn't need him for his money or his status—she had her own. And yet she wanted him. In a way that Ballard had never thought he'd be wanted. It was the way he thought his grandmother wanted his grandfather.

With that thought, his hips increased speed, his release near to bursting free. Janelle had grabbed the backs of her legs, lifting them higher to increase the depth of his penetration. They were both moaning

and inching closer, waiting impatiently for the pleasure to claim them.

And when it did, as their bodies convulsed and
relaxed, Ballard looked into her eyes and said, as
simply as if he were asking her name, "Marry me."

"Excuse me?" Janelle asked, pulling her legs down
and sliding back on the bed.

She grabbed the sheets to cover her exposed body,
because if he'd just said what she thought he'd just
said, they were about to have a conversation that
didn't lend itself to nakedness.

"Marry me," he repeated.

She watched him carefully to see if maybe he
hadn't been sure he'd really said that in the first place
either. But there was only the look of expectation.
In fact, he sat up next to her, reaching for her hand.
She almost didn't give it to him, but he was lacing
his fingers through hers as she continued to blink at
him with a look she knew had to be full of confusion.

"Listen, you're a terrific woman. You're beautiful and intelligent. You're running a successful business and you're one of the classiest females I know.
There's so much I admire about you, from your loyalty to your family and friends to your professional-
ism with your clients."

She opened her mouth to speak, but he continued,
pressing forward like a freight train.

"We're more compatible than most married cou-
ples we both know and considering the line of work
you're in, I'm sure you can attest to that. We come

from similar backgrounds, our roots grounded in our family businesses or at least the knowledge of working hard to achieve your dreams. We're both establishing those dreams, independent and on our way to doing even bigger things. We know what we want out of life and how to pursue it. There's really no reason we shouldn't get married."

This time Janelle did try to pull her hand away from his grasp, but he held firm.

"And besides, once my family announces that they're backing your father in the election, we'll already be connected in the political arena. We might as well make it official all the way around," he finished.

When he looked at her then, he even had the audacity to appear proud of himself, as if he'd just presented the case of the century and there was no way she could refute him.

"You cannot be serious," she said finally. "You're asking me to marry you and we've known each other not quite two months now."

"I just drove thirty minutes to get to your house in the middle of the night," he told her pointedly. "Now I'm sitting on your bed naked after what might actually be the best sex I've ever had, and you're commenting on how well we know each other."

"This is sex, Ballard," she refuted. "It's been sex since the first two dates, remember? That's the way this works for you."

He was quiet for a second, thinking, just as she was.

"Is that all it's really been, Janelle? Are you honestly telling me that after your no-dating stance, you just decided to simply have sex with me?"

Well, now that he put it that way... "That's not what I'm saying. I just think this might be rather quick. And as you said, the sex just now was *really* good. Maybe you were just in the moment or something." God, she hoped so. Otherwise, what the hell was she going to say?

He used his other hand to tilt her chin upward so that they were staring eye to eye. "I've never asked another woman to marry me before. I've never even considered being married or having a family, not until you."

As far as words went, those weren't so bad, Janelle thought. They weren't exactly what she thought she should be hearing when a man asked her to marry him, but they weren't as bad as *I'm glad I'm not marrying you* either. More cruel words Janelle thought she'd never hear again.

Still, none of that gave her an idea of what her answer should be or if she should even be considering this offer at all.

Ballard didn't give her another minute to contemplate, but moved in closer to her, touching his lips softly to hers.

This she could do, Janelle thought as she let her eyes flutter closed, accepting the softness of his mouth against hers, the warmth of their tongues slipping and sliding along each other as they seemed to enjoy doing.

She didn't allow herself to think of the question

again, didn't want to contemplate, wanted only to feel. It had been so long since she'd *felt* or since she'd let feelings guide her and she was long past due. So she wrapped her arms around Ballard's neck, let him pull the covers away from her and they lay down together, kissing, moaning, loving each other, even if only in the physical sense, once more.

## Chapter 13

"I'm getting married," Janelle announced on Monday as they sat at the Quarterdeck finishing off their after-dinner glasses of wine. "Next week," she finished when neither Vicki nor Sandra said a word.

She drank the last little bit of her wine, letting the words hang in the air as her two best friends stared at her wide-eyed, questions undoubtedly rolling through their minds but not quite able to be spoken just yet.

As she set her glass on the table, she nodded. "I know just how you feel. I felt that way myself the first few moments after Ballard popped the question. It took some cajoling and some…ah…convincing that this was the logical next step for us. But now I'm game and I haven't been able to think of anything else since. I finally get to plan my wedding! Can you believe that? I thought I'd forgotten what I wanted all those years ago, but I didn't, and I cannot wait to get started. We don't have much time. Did I tell you it's in a week?"

"Stop. Stop. Stop," Vicki protested, holding up a hand and leaning over the table to stare at Janelle. "Are you serious?"

"I think she is," Sandra replied blandly. "The real question should maybe be, are you out of your damned mind?"

Janelle laughed. She'd known that question would come from one of them at some point.

"Does your father know? Is this about the election? Because it's only two weeks away and the polls indicate that he's got the lead over Windom, so I don't think you need to go this far to win," Vicki told her matter-of-factly.

"I'm not out of my mind," Janelle said, looking directly at Sandra. Then, switching her gaze to Vicki, she continued, "I haven't told my father yet. Having dinner with him and DJ day after tomorrow. And the Dubois family had already decided to endorse Dad, so that's not why we're doing this."

Sandra watched Janelle through narrowed eyes. "Okay, well, since you opened up that can, why *are* you two doing this? You said he proposed? When? Why so soon? Are you pregnant?"

Janelle's smile slipped. "Not funny. You know how obsessive I am about using birth control."

"Even though you weren't dating, yes, we know," Vicki added with a roll of her eyes. "But you have to admit this is weird for that fact alone. It's out of the blue and it just doesn't ring true. I mean, do you love him? Does he love you?"

Janelle didn't want to answer either of those questions. She was prepared for anything else they asked or assumed, but not that.

"Look, it's the right thing to do for us. Every couple is different and we know what we want. So do I have a dress designer and a florist or should I start looking for vendors?"

"You should probably start looking for your common sense since you have obviously lost it," Sandra quipped.

Janelle frowned. "Oh, I see. It was fine for me to sleep with him and—what did you say?—'leave if necessary'? But I can't possibly marry him. He can't possibly want to marry me of all people, the uptight and boring one of the Silk Sisters."

Silence immediately followed her heated words and Janelle felt bad, sort of. These were her friends. They were supposed to support her, not look at her as though she'd broken four or five laws and was headed to death row.

"Come on, it's my wedding," she said quietly. "Are we really going to argue about this?"

Sandra finished off her drink, set the glass down and frowned toward the window, then looked back at Janelle. "I'm going to say this because I'm your friend and I love you, and I know you're not going to like it."

She gave Janelle a moment to object. Janelle remained silent.

"Don't feel like you have to marry the first guy to ask you since Jack. You're a terrific woman. You're not frigid and you're not boring, despite what that asshole said and did to you. That was all about him, Janelle. You were the best thing to ever happen to his sorry ass. And you deserve the very best. That's all I want for you."

Vicki joined in as soon as Sandra finished. "That's all *we* want for you."

Reaching her hands across the table, Janelle smiled at her friends. When their fingers were entwined, she told them with all the honesty she absolutely felt at the moment, "I am happy. I know it seems strange and out of character for me, but this is what I want to do. It's what I need to do for myself for a change. And it's going to be terrific once we finally start planning."

In seconds they were all smiling, all grasping each other's hands and silently committing to this wedding, to this joining, no matter what they might be feeling on the inside.

"Okay, let's get started," Vicki said, digging into her purse for her notepad and pen.

Sandra followed suit, retrieving her iPad from her bag. Glad they'd now shifted to work mode, Janelle went into her own purse, then took out her tablet and pulled up the document she'd already begun working on regarding her wedding. That was what she'd titled the document—My Wedding. She'd never thought she'd be at this place, planning this event. Of all the events she'd ever planned, this one definitely had the most significance, the most emotional impact. Fighting back tears, she pushed her empty plate aside and was ready to begin.

"You love pink," Vicki began. "And orchids are your favorite."

"I still have the notes from our high school days," Sandra began. "I've kept a file for each of us separately, so I know exactly what type of dress you want."

Janelle cleared her throat. "I don't want any of that," she announced.

They both looked up at her in question.

"I have a totally different idea for my wedding now," she told them. "I'm not that same idealistic dreamer I was in high school and I'm certainly not the naive love-struck girl I was in college."

Sandra nodded her agreement. "You're right," she said. "Tell us what you have in mind."

With a smile, Janelle happily began, "The theme is…change. Times change, seasons change, and if they're smart enough and open to personal growth, people eventually change."

Vicki smiled. "All right, I'm intrigued."

Janelle turned her tablet so that they could both get a visual of what she'd come up with.

"Fall is my favorite season. I love the fresh crisp colors, the scent in the air, the buffer between the sultry days of summer and the cold snowy days of winter. I want to incorporate all those elements into a whimsical and celebratory experience."

Tapping her pen against the table, Vicki nodded.

"I can see it. Huge Tuscan planters filled with chrysanthemums, dahlias, spider mums."

"And tulips," Janelle added. "I want baby tulips because they have so much potential for cheeriness."

"Is that the Chancellor property?" Sandra asked, staring down at the tablet.

"Yes, I was thinking of going with a rustic-chic theme. We could transform the barn space so that it's elegant and play off the earthy charm at the same time." Excitement formed in the pit of Janelle's stomach like a slow storm, churning and brewing, waiting for the exact moment to break free. She was certain that moment would be the day she walked down that aisle and said "I do" to Ballard, to the man who would be her husband. The husband she never thought she would have.

"Oh, that's going to be lovely, Janelle. Just lovely!" Vicki purred.

Sandra was nodding again, this time going back into her bag to get her sketchpad. Pulling the pencil she kept tucked in the spiral top, she turned to a clean page and talked as she sketched, not looking up at them.

"You won't wear white, because change is good. Flip it a little and go with a peach or maybe even a very soft green, celadon, maybe. Halter, V-neck, simple yet chic. The perfect combination for Janelle Howerton!" Sandra happily lifted the quick sketch and showed it to Janelle.

Janelle did tear up then, the emotion filling her throat until she thought she might not be able to speak. "I love it!" she exclaimed. "I was thinking of a charcoal-gray-and-orange color scheme. Ballard looks fantastic in charcoal-gray. And you two can wear a soft gray dress."

"And you'll be the splash of color in a lovely shade of peach," Sandra said, confirming she was on board with the color scheme.

"I love it! This is going to be beautiful," Vicki exclaimed.

"Oh, my goodness, I can't believe you're the first one of us to get married," Sandra added with her own gleeful smile.

"I can't either," Janelle admitted. "But I'm really going to marry Ballard Dubois in exactly six days. So let's get ready to pull some all-nighters."

"With that said, we're going to need some champagne," Vicki announced.

"I'm with that," Sandra agreed, waving over one of the waiters. After she ordered champagne and the waiter came back with two chilled bottles and three glasses, they all held their glasses up for a toast.

"To the first of the Silk Sisters to walk down the aisle," Sandra began.

"To Janelle's happily-ever-after," Vicki followed up.

"To new beginnings and taking chances," Janelle finished, and as they clinked glasses, bringing them to their lips for their first sips of the chilly bubbly liquid, words echoed in Janelle's mind.

*To love.*

\* \* \*

"Your plane ticket, sir," Lucy, Ballard's secretary for the past six years, said, placing an envelope down on his desk.

He barely looked up, he was so focused on quarterly reports and storage contracts. Building their own warehouse was the best decision he'd ever made. He could be proud of that fact. His father had disagreed, believing that the tax breaks they would get from using city-owned facilities would work out more to their advantage. But that wasn't true and those tax breaks were contingent on which politician was in office at what time. For Ballard that was too much of a gamble. So not only were they now getting New York offices, but just yesterday they'd broken ground on the spot where their new warehouse would be built.

"A car will be waiting for you at the airport and your room at the Ritz-Carlton is already booked."

He heard Lucy talking, knew she was saying something about the impromptu trip to Miami he was making and figured since she was now silent, he should say something. "Thanks, Lucy."

Ballard thought he would hear the close of his office door next, signaling that Lucy had left, but instead he heard her clearing her voice.

"Yes?" he said, finally looking up at the pleasant middle-aged female. "Was there something else?"

"I believe congratulations are in order," she said, her ruby-coated lips twitching in a smile. "You were in meetings all day yesterday when I read the announcement in the morning paper, so I didn't have a chance to speak to you."

Ballard crossed his hands over the many reports spread out on his desk and smiled up at her. "Thank you."

Lucy shook her head. "I just can't believe you're finally taking the plunge. Would have never guessed you'd get married," she continued.

That had been the gist of what his father had said when he'd told him and his grandparents, as well. His mother was currently in Sicily, so he'd sent her an email. She'd replied this morning with her congratulations and promised to be back by the ceremony on Sunday. As for his future family, he'd be meeting with them tomorrow night.

Ballard turned his wrist, looked at his watch and figured he'd better wrap things up here. He didn't want to miss his flight.

This trip was too important.

At nine-thirty the next morning, Ballard walked into the corporate offices of Trell Cosmetics.

"If you don't have an appointment, Mr. Trellier will not be able to see you," said the tall, exotic beauty seated behind the glass desk, pink walls with the word *Trell* scripted in gold letters behind her.

Ballard slipped both hands into his pockets, pushing his suit jacket back to give her a full, unfettered view. Then he smiled and waited while she absorbed everything.

"I'm an old friend and I'm in town for a couple of hours. If he's not in yet, I can wait in his office."

She watched him carefully, her long lashes moving up and down as she surveyed everything from the gold Movado at his wrist to the cuff links on his shirt, down to the tie of his Gucci shoes and back up to his face. He suspected she'd been calculating what everything was worth, giving her a general estimate of whether or not she should waste her time on him. The slow spread of her dark pink-painted lips across brilliant white teeth meant he'd added up satisfactorily.

"I'll walk you to his office, Mr..." Her voice trailed off as she stood and sashayed—that was the best word he could come up with to describe how she moved—over to stand next to him.

"Dubois," he filled in for her, and offered her his arm.

She took it, as he'd known she would, lacing hers through his and being sure to keep her body close to his as they walked down the short hallway to what could only be Jack Trellier's office.

After two unsuccessful attempts at "keeping him company" the gorgeous receptionist finally left him alone, proving that brains didn't always come with beauty, no matter how sexist that sounded. Luckily for her, he wasn't interested in anything in Trellier's office. He couldn't actually care less what went on with the day-to-day cosmetics business. What he knew for certain was that all this gold-and-pink would give him a headache and probably some type of complex if he had to be surrounded by it day in and day out.

Still, he thought as he moved to one of the windows, looking out across glistening Miami beach, Trell was at the top of its game and much of that credit went to the pretty-boy CEO.

Unfortunately, that pretty boy might not be so pretty after Ballard left this office today.

"I'm shocked someone as versed in business etiquette as yourself would neglect to make an appointment."

Ballard turned slowly at the sound of Trellier's voice. He took his time taking a few steps toward the guest seats in the man's office, then decided against taking a seat at all. And since this wasn't a pleasure visit, he decided it was best to simply get right to the point.

"Speaking of etiquette, I think you may have missed a few lessons in learning how to deal with an ex," Ballard told him.

Trellier, who was dressed in a very nice ivory-colored linen suit, a teal shirt beneath the jacket and camel suede loafers, kept moving until he was behind his marble-top desk. He removed his suit jacket and sat down.

"I know how to deal with all the women in my life. Maybe you need some lessons. I ran into Alaya at a party last week and she did not have pleasant things to say about you."

He smiled as he talked but Ballard wasn't amused.

"I don't give a damn what she has to say. I'm only concerned with one woman and you seem to have fixated on her again all of a sudden. I want it to stop," he said quietly, yet deadly serious.

This apparently amused Trellier because he laughed, loudly. The sound irritated Ballard and his fingers curled at his sides.

"She's not worth all this you know," Trellier said. "I mean, I'm assuming you haven't slept with her yet or you'd know for sure she wasn't worth the time. Look, I've just been having some fun where you two are concerned. Nothing serious, nothing for you to worry about. I'm not going to try to steal your girl, if that's what you're here to talk about."

Ballard shook his head. He moved until he was standing right up against Trellier's desk. "No, I'm not worried about you stealing my fiancée. You see, I'm very confident in the man I am. I don't need to blame a female for my shortcomings, nor do I need to assault one when I don't get what I want."

The smile that had been all over Trellier's face slipped slowly, surely, from his face. He sat back in his chair, folding his hands in his lap.

"I see she's decided to run her mouth. Still immature, still a liar. It's unfortunate that you chose to believe her."

Ballard smirked. "What's unfortunate is that you underestimate me."

"Is that supposed to be some type of threat?"

"Oh, no, it's a definite promise, Trellier. You keep going with these stories, you keep poking at Janelle and her father's campaign, and you will regret it."

"Ha! You cannot threaten me, Dubois. I have just

180     *Eve of Passion*

as much power as you, probably more since my face is all over the country, while yours is where? On a goddamned boat." He lifted a hand, waving Ballard away. "Go on back to your little Boston wedding. Marry the bitch, for all I care. She wasn't good enough for me five years ago and she's definitely not good enough now."

Refusing to rise to Trellier's bait, Ballard continued without flinching. "But her recollection of the sexual assault that occurred in Europe will be more than good enough for the authorities. And on the off chance that's not enough for you, I'm sure your customers—you know, the women that spend a fortune on your products—would be more than happy to hear what she has to say."

For the first time, and like an arrow to the bull's-eye, Trellier tensed. "Nobody will believe her. They'll want to know why she waited so long to talk."

"They'll be more interested in the fact that this wasn't your first time assaulting a female."

Trellier went absolutely pale at that moment.

"Janelle was down for anything I did to her. She wanted to please me, so she did whatever I asked. Except that one night and that was because she'd been talking to those stupid-ass girlfriends of hers all the time. They were always meddling, telling her what to do, what to say. She wanted it!" Trellier roared.

Ballard shook his head. "That's why Janelle fought you. It's why Natalie Jackson chased you out of her house with a knife. You're a piece of shit, Trellier. And if I had my way I'd be calling the police and a press conference to air all your dirty laundry. Lucky for you, I'm going to make you an offer you'd better not refuse."

Trellier looked to the window, a muscle ticking in his jaw. Then he looked back at Ballard. "What do you want?"

Punkass, Ballard thought with another shake of his head. Ready to assault females, but no backbone to fight for his reputation at all. No, he'd do whatever Ballard said, give him whatever he wanted to keep this from getting out. He wanted to punch him for just sitting there breathing.

"I don't want her name in your mouth, in your mind, not even in your freakin' search history—do you understand me? Not another picture, another story, another quote, nothing. Are we clear?"

"Whatever, man, she's just another bitch. You are being way too serious about all this."

Ballard had been so close to leaving, so close to just stating his case and walking the hell out of this disgustingly nauseating office. And then the jackass had opened his mouth one more time. Ballard was around the desk before he could think to stop himself. One punch, that was all it took and Trellier was sprawled on the floor.

"Her name is Janelle and she's about to become my wife. If you ever think about addressing her or referencing her again, it better be as Mrs. Dubois."

"Whatever, man, you broke my effing nose," Trellier whined.

Ballard was already walking out, the tape recorder

he'd slipped into the pocket of his jacket still rolling. The private detective he'd hired to find out everything there was to know about Trellier right after the dance had given him the information on Natalie Jackson. She'd never wanted to press charges either, but it was good information to have just in case. For the most part, Ballard had decided to respect Janelle and Ms. Jackson by not feeding this information to the police himself. But if Trellier ever grew a set of balls and actually came after Janelle again, Ballard had his almost confession on tape. And if that wasn't enough to get him arrested, he'd simply break his damned nose, again.

# *Chapter 14*

Dinner with Janelle, her father and brother had gone as well as could be expected. Actually, Ballard hadn't expected it to go badly at all. From the things Janelle had told him about her relationship with her father, he got the impression that Darren Howerton had been leaning on his daughter way too much in the past years. The moment she became Ballard's wife that would stop. He could understand her desire to take care of her father and help ease his grieving, but he was sure she'd done that and then some. Asking her to secure Ballard's and his family's support had been a little over-the-top in Ballard's estimation. Especially since Howerton knew his father—he could have simply asked for support himself.

In retrospect, he may not have been in the position he was now—about to be married to a terrific woman—if Darren Howerton hadn't thought to impose on his daughter one last time. So he'd swallowed that little bit of ire and moved on. It was Darren who had seemed a little stilted during dinner, but Janelle hadn't appeared to notice. As for DJ Howerton, he was happy for his sister, happy she would be getting out of the Howerton house, as he'd told Ballard just before they'd left.

"She's settled for being here, for running her business and taking care of Dad. She deserves so much more out of life," DJ had said as he and Ballard stood by Ballard's car. Janelle was packing an overnight bag, so the two men had a few moments alone.

"She says she's happy here," Ballard countered, unsure of how much he could actually learn from DJ.

"She's happy as long as Mom and Dad were happy. That's how Janelle is. If she thought it would make life easier for anybody else, that's what she did. But it's past time for her to live for her. You make her smile. You make her glow. I think you're good for her."

Ballard had shaken the man's hand after that, promising to give him a call the next time he was in New York.

Now he and Janelle were once again in his penthouse. She'd gone immediately into his bedroom to put her bag and purse down and he fixed them each a glass of wine and took them into the living room, where he removed his suit jacket and tie and waited for her.

"That was a lot less painful than I anticipated," she was saying when she came back out.

She'd removed her heels and now wore flat slipperlike socks on her feet. Her khaki slacks and pink blouse were all that were left of the day's attire. Even her hair, which had been pulled back in a loose bun at the nape of her neck, was now hanging free. She looked relaxed and comfortable and when Ballard let himself stare at her a second longer, he realized how comfortable and natural this scene appeared. Two successful adults, home after dinner, about to share a glass of wine and wind down for the night. Was this what they would do every night for the foreseeable future?

"Your brother seems like a nice guy," he said when it seemed he was taking too long to reply.

"DJ's a great guy. I wonder when some woman's going to come along and snap him up. I'd hate for him to spend all his time working," she said.

Ballard picked up the glass he'd set on the table, offering it to her as they both stood in front of the couch.

"Thanks," she replied before taking a seat.

Ballard sat, as well, but didn't pick up his glass. Instead he reached over to the coffee table and picked up the stack of papers that had been lying there. Clearing his throat because suddenly it felt very dry, he handed the papers to her.

"When you get a second, if you could just review and sign those."

Janelle nodded, bringing the glass to her lips for a sip as she looked down at the papers.

Ballard didn't look at her, but he wondered what she was thinking. What was going through her mind as she read the first paragraphs? How would she react? Would she sign? Would she refuse? Would the wedding be called off?

In the span of about twenty seconds all those questions ticked off in his mind, no answers, or rather, possible answers that made his heart beat faster, panic slipping down his spine in icy tendrils. He reached for the glass of wine and took a huge gulp before sitting back on the couch, still not looking at Janelle.

Out of the corner of his eye he could see her leaning forward to put her glass back on the table. She then got up, papers in hand, and went into the bedroom. Ballard resisted the urge to groan or to go after her, but he did pick up his glass again and empty the contents. This wasn't a business deal, he thought, possibly a tad too late. He should have talked to her about the agreement first, should have gotten her opinion and taken it into consideration before presuming this was the way to go. He'd have to approach things differently once they were married, to get used to the idea of discussing the important decisions between them instead of presenting them like another business deal.

He could do that, he thought, running his palms over his thighs. He'd graduated magna cum laude a year early; there was no reason he couldn't get the hang of this relationship thing in time to build a successful marriage. He could… Where the hell was she and what was taking her so long?

As if he'd conjured her, she appeared standing before him, extending the papers back to him. "Here you go," she said.

Ballard took the papers from her, relief washing over him like a waterfall. She'd signed them and there had been no argument, no hurt feelings and no rejection. He was just about to say something, to lean over and kiss her, possibly, take her to bed and make long, sweet love to her for the rest of the night. But he looked down at the papers first, and all movement, all coherent thought ceased.

"You had a prenuptial agreement drawn up?" he asked, a little more than astonished.

She sat beside him once more, watching as she held up the papers he'd given her. She wiggled them at him. "So did you. Great minds must think alike."

Ballard didn't know how he felt about this development. He hadn't for one second considered she might do this, that she'd even be thinking along those lines.

"You expect me to sign a prenup?" he asked, the words foreign to his ears.

"I guess we both expected each other to sign one. So I say we go over both, come up with our common points and have a new agreement drawn up in the morning. We'll both sign and move on. I was also thinking about where we would live today. This is a great place, but my business is in Wintersage. I know that yours is here, so we should probably talk about some common ground."

Common ground, she was saying. Ballard's temples throbbed. This was a relationship, correct? Just a few short minutes ago he'd feared he was handling this like a business deal. Now Janelle sounded as though she'd walked into the boardroom and had taken a seat right next to him at the conference table.

"So you're protecting your assets, just as I was protecting mine?" he asked, still not sure he understood exactly what was going on.

"Yes. It's smart for both of us. I mean, it's obvious we're not marrying each other for any type of business gain, but it would be irresponsible if we didn't even address it," she told him. She'd crossed her legs in the chair and was now flipping through the agreement. "Page one of yours looks good."

Ballard stood, dropping the papers she'd given him onto the coffee table. He rubbed a hand down the back of his head and went to stand at the window.

"We're getting married in three days," he said, looking out toward the night sky.

"Yes, it's just three days away. Did you get the email I sent earlier with the seating chart? It's been a madhouse at the office with all three of us working double time with our own clients and then doing things for this wedding. Sandra's freaking out that my dress may not be done in time. I told her it was okay—I was sure I had something in my closet I could wear instead," she said with a chuckle.

"I saw the email. My grandparents confirmed with all their friends and are going out today to find the perfect dress for my grandmother. Oh, I added my secretary to the guest list. I forgot to tell you." He was talking but he wasn't thinking. No, he was thinking but what he was thinking didn't seem to be in line with what they were doing. Something inside him said this was wrong, that this was not how things should be going. He'd had a plan, a set of events that would lead them down the aisle to an agreeable union, but this—it just didn't seem right. He frowned, then turned back to look at her.

"That's fine. We have a few extra spaces because my uncle and his wife are on a Mediterranean cruise and won't be back in time. You know Brenda, my event assistant that you met at the homecoming dance. She stopped by the office today with two magazines. I wanted to scream when she dropped them onto my desk but then I looked inside and saw the nicest picture of us. It was when we went to lunch the other day at the Quarterdeck. I swear these reporters must hide in the bushes. I never see them the way I do on TV, thrusting cameras in celebrities' faces all the time. Not that I'm complaining, just observing," she finished, and flipped to another page of the papers he'd given her. "We're covering the same ground here. I think it'll be simple for our attorneys to merge this into one document. I don't need any type of settlement and you're not asking for one, so it should be simple."

But it wasn't simple, Ballard thought, looking over at her. Nothing about this moment, these past few days, was as simple as he'd thought they would be when he asked her to marry him. It had been the most logical decision and yet…now he was having second thoughts. He couldn't pinpoint why, just a feeling in his gut that wasn't sitting well, an urge to do something differently that he wasn't sure he should dismiss.

She refolded the papers and set them on the table. "This is done." She stood and came over to him, wrapping her arms around his waist. "You look stressed. Is everything okay at work?"

"Yes," he replied after a few seconds, loving the feel of her arms around him. She'd done this on more than one occasion this past week, holding him against her as if she needed him there. "Everything's fine," he told her, wrapping his own arms around her shoulders. "Construction is under way. They're working on an expedited schedule in an effort to beat the winter weather. I don't think there's anything to worry about but I've got my best site manager heading to New York in the morning. He'll keep me posted while we're away the next two weeks."

"I can't wait to get away," she said, resting her cheek against his chest. "I don't usually like surprises but I'm excited about heading off to a secret honeymoon location."

"So am I," Ballard responded, lifting a hand to run down the back of her head, his fingers tangling in the soft strands of her hair.

He held her tightly, closing his eyes to the warmth spreading throughout him at her touch. Or was the warmth spreading throughout him for another reason? Of course he wanted to make love with her— that need never seemed to ebb. Instead it built at an alarming rate each time he heard her voice, saw her face. They'd been together more this week than any-time during their short romance, and it hadn't really seemed like enough.

"Hey," she said, looking up at him. "Let's hop in the hot tub. I keep peeking into that room each time I'm here. Since we may or may not continue stay-ing here, I'd like to have a turn in there. What do you think?"

Ballard looked down at her, stared into the light brown eyes he'd grown accustomed to looking at, saw the little mole at the corner of her right eye. Her lips were just about bare of lipstick or the gloss she pre-ferred to wear and yet they were all the more enticing to him. When they spread into a smile, he felt as if someone had punched him straight in the gut, and he almost buckled under the pressure. Instead he smiled in return, leaning down to kiss the tip of her nose.

"Your wish is my command," he replied.

When Janelle climbed on top of him, her breasts swollen, nipples hardened and just a breath away from his mouth, Ballard realized just how good an idea this hot tub escapade was.

The warmth of the water bubbling around their naked bodies had only stirred him more. As she low-ered herself slowly onto his erection, he closed his eyes to the sensations rippling through his body, the thoughts prickling his mind.

"Look at me," she whispered, settling her hips over him until he was buried deep inside her. She could have asked him to rob a bank or jump off a mountain at this moment and Ballard would have gladly done it.

He opened his eyes to stare up at her, wrapping his arms around her waist and holding her tightly as his hips jutted upward of their own accord.

"I want you to watch me, to know that in just three days we'll be like this forever," she whispered, taking her bottom lip between her teeth as she raised up slightly, then came down over his length once more.

Ballard swallowed, his gaze fixated on her. He did lift his hands to push her hair back from her face, holding it there as she began a slow, tortuous rhythm of up and down, around and repeat. He picked up the rhythm, meeting her stroke for delicious stroke.

"It will be just like this," he told her. "Just you and me."

"Yes," she whispered. "Yes."

He kissed the damp skin of her chest, his tongue lapping up the drops of water that settled between her breasts. She held on to the back of his head, picking up the pace of their rocking motion, pleasure building until Ballard was breathless. His palms flattened on her back, slipped down to grip her bottom as he drove deeper inside of her, ready for the explosion that burned against his scrotum.

"Forever, Ballard. We'll be like this forever," she declared, her voice shaking as her release took over.

As her thighs quaked around him, Ballard's body tensed, the word *forever* echoing in his mind as his own release ripped free, their bodies remaining locked together in the bubbling water.

# Chapter 15

The Wintersage Maritime Museum was the perfect location for Darren Howerton's final political event before the election. In another week, they would all be gathered here one more time to watch the results roll in from the polls.

All around the perimeter of Seventh Street, media vans were set up with their satellites positioned to broadcast this event throughout the state and, in the case of the CNN van that had pulled up in the early morning hours, nationally.

In a half hour the museum doors would open and all the guests who had checked into local hotels and B and Bs would pour inside, not paying a bit of attention to the rich history of Wintersage displayed through paintings and artifacts throughout the three-story redbrick building. Janelle's staff had done very little to decorate the area, partially because of the town ordinances that prohibited her from doing so, and because she hadn't felt it was needed. High tables had been strategically placed, covered in tablecloths that coordinated with her father's navy-blue-and-white campaign colors. On each table was a ceramic rendition of a ballot box, the Howerton name checked off, with a votive candle inside. Selia DuVane had made the boxes and would be selling them throughout the week in her shop.

Vicki had also thought the less-is-more strategy was best and had potted live plants posted throughout on each floor. At the welcome table, where "Vote for Howerton" buttons, bumper stickers and lawn posters would be handed out, was an arrangement of blue, white and green carnations, one of which her father wore tucked into the lapel of his navy blue suit jacket.

Tonight, even though she was semiworking the event, Janelle had foregone her usual black and also wore navy blue, a knee-length pencil skirt and jacket with a white shell beneath. She checked her watch once more, wondering if Ballard would make it on time. He'd said he had a meeting that started about half an hour ago, so they weren't entirely sure he'd be here at all. She hoped he would be.

It was no secret, at least to her, that the marriage proposal that had come out of the blue had morphed into something much bigger. She had feelings for Ballard Dubois. Were they love? She hadn't slapped that label on them yet, because the last time she had, she'd been horribly wrong. Still, her heart thumped each time she thought of him, her body warmed whenever he was near and she missed him like crazy when he was away. Every thought in her mind for the past week had revolved around him, their wedding, their future. She knew that nobody believed Ballard loved her, that they all thought this might be a marriage of convenience, but she didn't care. For so long she'd done what she thought everyone else wanted her to do. She'd lived the life that was easiest, without any emotional conflicts. She'd settled, as DJ had told her just before last night's dinner. It didn't happen often, but she was inclined to agree with her brother's words.

But in two days she would be Mrs. Ballard Dubois. She would have someone to go home to at night who wasn't her father, somewhere to live that wasn't the empty house she shared with him. She'd have someone to build on her hopes and dreams with who wasn't one of her childhood friends who already knew those hopes and dreams by heart. There was no explaining her excitement, no explaining the reason she didn't believe that marrying Ballard was just another form of settling. There was no explanation because she didn't feel the need to make one and luckily for her, the people who loved her hadn't pushed for one.

Well, at least not all of them.

"Are you in love with him?" her father had asked abruptly when he'd come into the room a few moments ago.

She'd jumped at the sound of his voice, so entrenched in her thoughts that she hadn't heard his approach. Turning to face him now, she squared her shoulders, ready for this confrontation that she should have known would come.

"This wedding is extremely important to me, Dad. I would venture to say as important as this election is to you," was her reply.

"That's not what I asked you," he said, walking slowly toward her.

He looked so studious and sort of foreboding with his shining shoes and expertly cut suit. She could smell his cologne and fought off the stabs of homesickness that poked at her. He was a tall man with broad shoulders and coffee-toned skin, the salt-and-pepper of his hair and beard lending a distinguished air to the man she knew possessed a heart of gold. If her mother were here, she would be so proud to see him come to this point. Win or lose, Darren Howard was a successful man and she was very proud of him.

"It's not like you and Mom, if that's what you're getting at," she replied with a sigh. "We didn't see each other across a crowded town picnic and decide it was love at first sight. We weren't sweethearts for four years while she went to college and you into the navy. I tried that type of relationship and it didn't work out for me."

"I'm not making a comparison, baby girl. I'm just asking you a simple question." He reached up, tucked a strand of hair behind her ear.

Janelle turned to look out the window once more. "I like being with him. We have a lot in common."

"And that's a good foundation," Darren told her. "But is it enough to sustain a marriage? Should you be taking more time to get to know him, to see where this will lead?"

"I gave Jack Trellier four years and that didn't lead anywhere but to heartache. Excuse me if I'm no longer on the take-my-time bandwagon." Janelle sighed once more after that remark. It had been bitchy and probably unnecessary, but she didn't want to have this conversation, not now and certainly not with her father.

"This is what I want to do. It's what will make me happy," she told him, turning to face him.

He smiled then, touching his hands to her shoulders. "Then that's all that matters," he said. "Your happiness has always been what mattered most to me."

There had been so many times over the years that Janelle had doubted that statement. Standing here at this moment, she wondered if that had been her own selfishness, or if her father had also lost sight of that fact. Either way, this was where they were now. They both needed to function from this point forward.

"I can't wait for you to walk me down that aisle," she said, smiling up at him, feeling like the little girl who'd just given him her honor roll report card.

Darren pulled her close for a tight embrace. "And I cannot wait to see how beautiful you will be on your wedding day."

"I love you, Daddy," Janelle admitted, wrapping

her arms around her father, feeling as though they'd finally met on common ground.

Darren seemed to let out a whoosh of air, his arms tightening around her. "I love you, too, baby girl. I'll always love you."


"Do you love my daughter?" Darren Howerton asked Ballard just ten minutes before Ballard was due to take the podium to make his announcement.

Ballard fastened the single button on his suit jacket as he stood in front of the man who would soon become his father-in-law. He had a lot of respect for Darren Howerton, for the technology conglomerate the man had built on his own, for the loving marriage he'd had until his wife's death and for the two great children he'd raised. If there were some feelings of discord over what Ballard felt was a selfish misstep on Darren's part, well, Ballard had already decided that he would let that rest. He had no intention of calling the man out for attempting to use his daughter for political purposes. Or at least he thought that was the plan.

"I plan to marry your daughter in two days," was Ballard's steady response.

Darren nodded. He looked around the crowded room. The event was in full swing, had been for the past hour and fifteen minutes. Political supporters, local officials and some of what he now knew was Wintersage's upper class were all gathered here tonight to kick off the last round of campaigning for one of their own. Ballard had arrived only about twenty minutes late and had immediately found Janelle doing what she did best during events—directing and handling her business.

He'd been immediately elated to see her and had shown it in a way that before now he'd been against, publicly. His arms had laced around her waist from behind as he'd leaned in and kissed her neck while whispering, "Hello." She'd reciprocated by turning into his embrace and giving him a hello kiss on his lips. A more public display of affection he had never participated in—aside from their sidewalk kiss in Beacon Hill a few weeks ago—and he knew they could expect a huge picture in tomorrow's paper.

"I know when the wedding is. I have a personal invitation," Darren replied, his cordial political smile in place.

Ballard followed his cue, having just been thinking about all the press that was milling about. He relaxed so that his facial expression would appear cordial, as well, no matter what he was feeling on the inside.

"Janelle is very important to me, Mr. Howerton. I want only the best for her."

"And you believe you're the best for her?"

"I believe I may be the only one, at the moment, with Janelle's best interests in mind."

Darren chuckled then. "Are you trying to tell me something?"

The correct answer would be no. Just as the correct action where Jack Trellier had been concerned might have been to stay away from the guy and let his lawyers take care of him. But Ballard had handled that himself and knew without another thought he would do the same here. Janelle was going to be his wife, so it was his job to protect her from all harm. He planned to take that job very seriously.

"I'm simply saying that asking her to date a man for your political gain may not have been with her best interest in mind," he told Darren.

For a slight second there was a frown. Darren looked down at the floor and when he looked up again, his smile was once again in place. "I didn't tell her to fall for you and I certainly didn't expect you to take advantage of her. I admit now that I should have rethought what I was asking her to do." He took a deep breath, released it and continued. "I would rather you not take that stage to announce your support of me if you're not marrying my daughter for the right reasons."

Because, despite his previous acts, Darren Howerton loved his daughter very much. Ballard hadn't really doubted that fact, just as he didn't doubt that at one time his own father had loved his mother and him. The problem was that for all these rich and powerful men could build empires and manage thousands, they had the hardest time simply being honest with and respecting the people closest to them.

"Dubois Maritime Shipping is backing the Howerton campaign because we believe in your platform and that you can make positive changes in Washington. We would have given this support without the involvement of your daughter, sir," Ballard told him just as Darren's campaign manager took the podium.

In the next few seconds Ballard heard his name being called and he turned to walk out onto the stage. Darren's hand on his shoulder stopped him.

"Take good care of her," Darren said. "She deserves unconditional love and respect and happiness. She's given up too much of herself not to have those things."

Ballard only nodded his response and walked out to greet the crowd, to stand up for what would in a couple of days be his extended family.

On Sunday afternoon at two o'clock, two hundred guests sat in oak chivari chairs lined in straight rows up and down two sides of the Chancellor barn house. The space had long ago ceased being used to shelter animals and had recently sat empty until two years ago when Rob Chancellor retired from the firefighters and Janelle planned his retirement party there. She had no idea at the time that she would redesign this entire space to become the wedding of her dreams.

White twinkle lights were draped throughout the rafters, wrapped in peach-colored netting accompanied by huge peach-colored satin bows. Down the center aisle, which was roped off at both ends, a long ecru runner stretched. Orange tulip petals littered the path. The altar was against an ecru-and-peach silk backdrop, adorned with pillar candles, candelabra, a host of different-sized white and orange pumpkins, and a table full of things significant to her and Ballard's relationship.

She'd selected the items herself. The domino mask

she'd worn the first night she met him, a napkin from the restaurant in the hotel where they'd shared their first dinner, the tube of lip gloss she'd been wearing the night he first kissed her, a rendition of the sign with the name of Ballard's yacht, *Simplicity,* scribed on it, the menu from After Four, and in the center of all the mementos was an eleven-by-seventeen picture of them dancing at the Wintersage homecoming. She'd managed to secure that from the local newspaper photographer who'd snapped it that night.

Forty minutes before the ceremony, she'd walked through the space one more time, checking the flowers and the runner, the programs and the music. This wedding had been planned in a week. It shouldn't be out of the norm for her to check everything twice before she could relax. Just as it was also customary for her to be nervous. So why was Vicki knocking softly on the bathroom door in her second attempt to hurry her out?

"Do you need any help, honey?" she was asking again.

Janelle had insisted on putting on her dress by herself. In all her dreams about her wedding her mother was the one to help her slip into the white lace and satin. Now her mother wasn't here. And her dress, just for the record, was a gorgeous shade of peach that draped over her hips and down to her knees, where it flared out in a darker shade into the train that flowed three feet behind her.

She loved the deep plunging neckline and the splash of bling at the center—the brooch her grandmother had given to her mother on her wedding day. Now, staring into the floor-length mirror they'd had to bring into the bathroom, she touched her hand to that brooch, looking at herself and wondering what the hell she was actually doing here.

In the distance she could hear the string quartet she'd hired playing mellow music, which signaled the guests were starting to arrive.

"I'm fine," she answered Vicki finally. "I'll be out in just a minute."

She would, she promised herself. Not only had she accepted Ballard's proposal, but she'd had her friends dedicate their entire week to getting ready for this event. They'd run every vendor they knew and every volunteer of the town ragged with the special requests and preparations. She'd stood beside her father at his political event just two days ago, smiling in a picture that featured her, her father, her brother and her future husband.

There was no backing out now.

Besides, she'd never do that again. One almost wedding in a lifetime was enough.

She moved to the door, slowly turned the lock and was just about to leave when a cold shiver went down her spine. *Ignore it,* she told herself, and remembered the last time she'd ignored a warning signal like that. Jack had shown up at the homecoming dance.

With a sigh, Janelle leaned into the door, resting her forehead on the buffed wood, and closed her eyes. She could do this, she told herself in between deep breaths. She had to do this. It wasn't only about her;

there were hundreds of people out there, including the man she finally admitted to herself that she loved.

It would have been a perfect day to go along with the perfect venue and perfect dress, if only he loved her back.


Ballard Dubois did not get nervous.

When he was five years old and climbed onto his first bike, after insisting that Oz, their butler, remove the training wheels, he was not nervous as he pressed on the pedals for the first time. When he was fourteen and the sixteen-year-old Mackenzie Lewis drank too much of the liquor in her father's room at the country club and pushed him into a dark closet, pulling his pants down, Ballard wasn't nervous at all.

Today, as he retied his bow tie for the third time, he wondered if he might finally be experiencing the elusive emotion.

"Here, let me help you," his mother said, coming into the small room he'd been given to get dressed.

He turned to greet her, hugging her the way he always did when he saw her, which was usually a couple times a year. After the divorce she became as scarce in his life as he supposed his father had been in hers. He'd dealt with that situation pretty much the same way he'd dealt with everything else in his life that wasn't about business: he'd moved on and let it be. Now, pulling back from her and looking into the familiar face of the woman who had raised him, he vowed that his children would never experience this type of distance with him.

His children? When did he decide that he wanted children?

"When did you get in?" he asked, letting his mother take over the bow tying for now.

"Last night. I'm staying at the cutest bed-and-breakfast down by the water. This is a lovely little town. I'm sure Janelle's going to hate having to move to the city," Gina Dubois stated.

She had the same complexion as Janelle, her black hair cut in a short and brash style he would not have associated with her. In fact, she looked bright and relaxed and happy, he thought. After all these years, she finally looked happy.

"She won't have to move into the city. I purchased a house for us here," he said, diverting his gaze from her to glance at his watch.

He didn't want to be late, but he wasn't certain he should be here at all.

Gina smiled, resting her palms on his chest after she'd finished the tie. "You bought a house so she wouldn't have to leave her home."

Ballard shrugged. "It made sense. I can drive in to work and I'll still have the condo there in case we want to get away and spend some time in the city."

"Because you want her to be happy and being here with her family and running her business makes her happy," she continued.

Ballard thought about her words, heard the weight of them lingering in the room. "Yes. I want to make her happy."

"That's good," she said, cupping his cheek with

one hand. "That's very good. Don't lose sight of that goal, Ballard. Never stop wanting to make her happy."

"I don't plan to desert her for business like Dad did with you."

Gina shook her head. "Don't even think about that. There was so much more falling apart with your father and me. Anyway, I want you to have a better marriage, a happier union, with Janelle. Can you do that?"

Could he?

The New York offices would require a lot of his attention. He'd have to travel a lot in the upcoming months. Then there was the deal his grandfather had made with him. After today he would be named CEO of the company. That would take even more of his time because he would have to focus on doing a good job. Could he do that and be here with Janelle, attend some of her events to help when she needed it, take her away when they both needed a vacation?

Could he really be a husband to her?

Could he love her?

The questions continued as the knock on the door signaled his father and grandfather's arrival. The two men who would be standing at the aisle with him as he took his vows. The reunion between Daniel and Gina was cordial and stiff, while his mother happily went into Hudson's arms, hugging him as if she'd missed him most.

Ten minutes later Ballard was standing at the altar, looking out on all the guests who had come to this small town to see him marry Janelle Howerton. In the back he spotted two news crews, the only two that had been invited to attend. He and Janelle had decided it was better to grant a little access instead of having them all camp out hanging from the trees to get a picture. There would be more at the reception, which would take place in what used to be the horses' stables on this multiacre property. Ballard stood tall, barely listening to the music playing in the background, hands clasped in front of him.

Vicki and Sandra walked down the aisle dressed in light gray dresses. Then the prettiest little girl came running down, dropping more tulip petals to the floor. Ballard wondered if one day he would have a little girl as cute as she or possibly as lovely as Janelle. He wondered about their future, about what they could both expect out of this arrangement.

It was an arrangement, wasn't it?

Hadn't that been what he'd proposed?

No, it was the logical solution—that was what he'd said to her. But as she made her appearance at the end of the aisle and began her descent, he wondered if that were enough, if that were fair to this woman whom he respected more than any other female he'd ever met.

She took steady steps, smiling at people she knew in the audience, getting closer to where he stood. Ballard unclenched his hands. She was beautiful in the colored dress, her complexion glowing in the contrast. He inhaled deeply. She was so close now he could smell her perfume. When she looked to his grandfather, her smile was bright and full. Then her gaze fell to his father, and her smile slipped. When she looked at Ballard, it disappeared completely.

And he knew.

This was a mistake. An awful mistake that he would have to compound just to fix.

Ballard took a step forward, hating the motion more than he hated himself at this moment. To his surprise, at the same time, Janelle took a step back, dropping her arm from her father's.

"Janelle," he said.

She shook her head.

The room was silent, the music droning on as everyone stared at them in question.

Ballard reached out his hand. "Come with me," he said. "Please."

"Ballard?" she whispered, her body poised to… to what? Run?

Ballard took the lead then, reaching for her hand and grabbing it in his. Then they were on the move, pushing past her father, her friends, heading toward the room where he'd gotten dressed only moments before.

## Chapter 16

"I can't do this," was the first thing Ballard said when they were alone in the room, the door closed behind them. "I can't marry you under these pretenses."

She looked devastated as he said the words, taking steps that backed her up against a wall of shelves. He wanted to reach for her, to hold her in his arms, but something stopped him. Guilt, most likely.

"I was wrong to propose to you, Janelle, wrong to suggest that we make a logical agreement to spend the rest of our lives together. I've been so used to doing business all my life that I just treated our relationship like another business arrangement."

Ballard turned away from her, the pain in his chest too great to continue looking at her as he spoke.

"I've always had a plan, always had specific steps

that I took to get where I needed to be. It's how I was raised, how I wanted my life to remain. Orderly, efficient, profitable—that's what I wanted. That's what I needed. Do you remember…" he said, turning around quickly in the hopes that she hadn't left him standing in there alone. On a sigh of relief he continued, "Do you remember that first night at dinner when you looked at me in horror as I talked about my dating method? You were angered because to you it sounded callous and impersonal. And you know what? It was. It's just taken me all these years to figure that out. No," he added with another sigh. "It took you coming into my life for me to figure it out. For me to figure out a lot of things." He rubbed his hands down his face, overwhelmed with everything moving inside of him at the moment. It felt like the tornadoes he watched on the Weather Channel, the huge funnel cloud touching down and wreaking all kinds of havoc and destruction—that was what his life had been like all these years and he hadn't even realized it. Then the bright sunny day that always appeared after the destruction. Today could have been that sunny day. It could have been the start of his new life, his new beginning, if only he'd been selfish enough to go through with it.

"I did all this for me," he told Janelle. "I proposed because I wanted you and I thought we should be together. I figured it was the most logical next step for us and I believed that with all my heart. On another level I think I proposed because my grandfather offered me the entire company if I married you."

He paused then, looking at Janelle as she stood in her wedding gown, staring at the woman who had changed his life.

"Then I thought of your father," he continued, "and how selfish it was of him to ask you to come to us for political support and I wanted to save you from him, from doing his bidding out of guilt. Then something happened, Janelle. Something I don't think I'll ever be able to explain.

"I went to Miami and broke Jack Trellier's nose. I changed my will. I bought us a house here in Wintersage because I didn't want you to leave your home. I tore up that infernal prenup because I wanted to give you everything I had, everything I was. I didn't know why I was doing those things, not until the moment I saw you walking down that aisle," he finished, looking across the room to where she still stood, blinking rapidly, breathing in deep, out fast.

He moved closer to her then, not sure if she would run out of the room or just punch him.

"I'm an idiot, a selfish idiot who made a huge mistake and I don't blame you if you hate me. I don't blame you if you walk out of here today and never want to see me again.

"But before you do, Janelle, before you decide, I want you to know that I love you. I've loved you all this time and was too pigheaded and too blinded by my own stupid logic to just admit it. I've never loved another woman and I'm likely not to experience this again at the rate I'm going. But I do love you, with all that I am, not all that I wanted to be or aspired to achieve, all that I am in here," he told her, tapping his hand over his chest.

When he was finished, when the weight from his shoulders had been lifted and he thought this moment would end with tears of happiness, or at least a modicum of compassion, there was only silence.

After another minute or so that stretched on like an hour—one of the most painful moments of his life—Ballard resigned himself to his fate.

"Whatever you do, don't be angry with yourself. You did nothing wrong. This is in no way a reflection of you. I am at fault and I will shout it to the world that I am a fool. Be good to yourself, Janelle, and be happy," he said before moving away from her, heading for the door.

His hand was on the handle when her voice stopped him.

"Ballard."

"All my life everyone has shielded me." Janelle began talking even while Ballard was still facing the door. "My parents, my brother. Even Sandra and Vicki tried to warn me about Jack, and after Jack they wanted me to date but only guys they approved. Everyone has to make decisions for Janelle, has to protect her. Protect me from what? From living my own life?"

She wasn't going to yell. It wasn't worth it. Was being embarrassed in front of two hundred people and the press worth it? she wondered.

"I knew exactly who you were when I first went

out with you. Sure, my father asked me to get the political backing for him, but did you think I wasn't smart enough to secure that and move on had that been what I really wanted to do? I'm not the naive, pathetic young girl Jack took advantage of. I'm a grown woman who knows what she wants in her life."

She turned then, saw that Ballard had not left but was now facing her with his back to the door.

"I knew when you asked me to marry you that wasn't the most romantic invitation. I knew you were looking at this union as something other than the love-filled relationship I'd always wanted."

He stepped forward, about to speak, but she held up a hand.

"No. You had your turn," she told him. "I knew all those things and I still agreed. I decided, Ballard—you did not convince me, nor did you persuade me. I decided to marry you because it was what I wanted. When Sandra and Vicki tried to talk me out of it, I told them this same thing. This is my life and I'm sick and tired of the people around me not believing I know how to live it."

"I'm sorry," he finally managed.

"Sorry for what? For going for what you wanted the way you always do? For pushing against my barriers and doing everything in your power to wake up the woman inside me that had been asleep for way too long? Or for being so pigheaded that you couldn't even see when things had begun to change between us, that you couldn't see when you'd begun to fall in love?"

The last was spoken quietly, her voice shaking a little as she said it. She'd hoped and she'd prayed that she was right, that his strange reaction to the prenup agreement had meant that he disagreed with yet another agreement between them. Those nights they made love, she'd wished for their physical communion to touch him on a deeper level, to open up the doors he didn't even know he'd kept closed because of his parents' failed marriage.

"I did all this," she said, waving a hand around her, "because I love you, Ballard, because no matter what, I believed in what we had together. If it was going to take you a while to finally get a clue, I was willing to wait."

"I shouldn't have made you wait a second," he said coming closer to her. "I was so foolish."

She smiled over the tears clogging her throat. "A foolish hero—who would have ever thought those words could describe your personality? Thank you for dealing with Jack. I wish I could have been there to see his nose breaking, his face filling with blood, the nasty bastard."

Ballard smiled then. He chuckled and reached for her this time, pulling her close to him and holding on tight.

"I love when you hold me like this," Janelle whispered as she wrapped her arms around his neck, holding him close, as well. "It's how I knew you had feelings for me, how I knew all your plans and logic were crumbling right before your eyes."

"You're one smart lady," he whispered, pulling

back far enough so he could kiss her. "One smart, sexy, enticing lady that I would be honored to have as my wife."

Then Ballard did something totally unexpected that gripped her heart like a vise. He went down on one knee, holding her hands in his.

"Janelle Howerton, I love you with every breath that I take. I cannot imagine what the next day, the next hour, the next second of my life would be without you. Will you please marry me, not because it's logical but because I need you?"

Her heart thumped. Sure, she was wearing a wedding dress and Ballard was wearing a tuxedo and just outside of this room were two hundred people wondering what the hell was going on. Still, this proposal, this heartfelt admission, brought tears to her eyes and joy deep down in her soul. She nodded because the words weren't coming as quickly as she would have liked.

"Yes, Ballard, let's go get married," she finally managed to say.

Now, this was a party, Sandra thought after leaving the dance floor. She'd been out there since the moment the bride and groom were officially announced, loving the joyous atmosphere and the huge smile of happiness on her best friend's face.

Janelle looked absolutely radiant, her gown a gorgeous masterpiece that would be all over gossip magazines and national papers by sunrise tomorrow morning. Success on the work front and happiness on the personal front—life was good.

"Come on, the bride's about to toss the bouquet," someone said as streams of single women made their way to the middle of the dance floor, preparing to catch the stunning throwaway bouquet Vicki had made for Janelle.

Speak of the devil, Vicki appeared beside her, resting a hand on her shoulder. "Hey, let's get out there. Janelle said she'd aim right at us."

Sandra shook her head. "Tell her to aim in another direction. All this happily-ever-after is not for me."

"Oh, come on, have some fun. You know that saying about the one who catches the bouquet being the next to get married is old superstition."

"Whatever, I'm not getting up there. You go right ahead and catch your Prince Charming," Sandra told her, then laughed as Vicki swished her happy behind up to the dance floor, pushing her way front and center so Janelle could see her.

The counting began and Sandra continued to laugh at all the women getting into their battle stances, preparing to catch that damned bouquet come hell or high water. Screams sounded as the bouquet was released and went soaring over the crowd. Soaring higher and farther than Sandra would have thought Janelle could throw, dropping with a disturbing plunk right into her lap. Shocked, Sandra grabbed the flowers to keep them from falling to the floor. Looking up, she heard the loud run of applause as everyone in the room now looked at her, the single woman who was sitting at her table minding her business and now holding that silly bouquet.

Sandra did the only thing she could do: she threw the damned thing back across the room, wishing the next unlucky female who caught it good luck and good riddance. And she ignored the raucous laughter that followed her actions.

\* \* \* \* \*

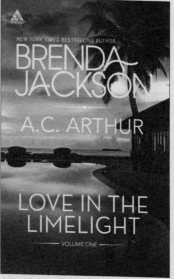

# REQUEST YOUR FREE BOOKS!

## 2 FREE NOVELS PLUS 2 FREE GIFTS!

KIMANI™ ROMANCE

### Love's ultimate destination!

KROM13R